The

Death of Ivan Ilyich

LEO TOLSTOY

The Death of Ivan Ilyich
by Leo Tolstoy

Translation by Robert Nesbit Bain
- - -

Published by Tribeca Books
ISBN 978-1936594665
Printed in the USA

Cover Design by SoHo Books

CHAPTER I

In the large building devoted to judicial business, during the interruption of the session in which the Meluisky affair was under consideration, the members of the Court and the Procurator had assembled in the cabinet of Ivan Egorovich Shebek, and were discussing the celebrated Krasovsky affair. Theodor Vasilevich, waxing warm, proved that there was no jurisdiction. Ivan Egorovich stuck to his opinion likewise. Peter Ivanovich, taking no part at first in the dispute, was simply glancing through the newspapers.

"Gentlemen!" said he, "Ivan Il'ich is dead."

"Impossible!"

"Read for yourselves, then, here it is," said he to Theodor Vasilevich, showing him the new number of the "Gazette," fresh and moist from the press.

Within a black border was printed: "Praskov'ya Thedorovna Golovina, with heart-felt regret, informs her relations and acquaintances of the death of her beloved husband and member of the High Court, Ivan Il'ich Golovin, which took place on the 4th of February of the current year. The funeral will take place at one o'clock in the afternoon."

Ivan Il'ich was a colleague of the gentlemen assembled there, and they all loved him. He had been ailing now for some weeks, and his malady was said to be incurable. His place had been left vacant, but the general impression was that, in case of his death, Aleksyeev might be nominated his successor, and either Vinnikov or Shtabel would take the place of Aleksyeev. Thus, on hearing of the death of Ivan Il'ich, the first thought of every one of the gentlemen assembled in that cabinet was: How would this death affect the members of the tribunal or their acquaintances in the way of change of position and promotion?

"Now I shall certainly get Shtabel's place or Vinnikov's," Theodor Vasilevich thought to himself. "It was promised to me a long time ago, and this promotion would mean an increment of 800 roubles, besides office fees."

"I must petition now for the transfer of my brother-in-law from Kaluga," thought Peter Ivanovich. "The wife will be very glad. Now she will not be able to say that I never do anything for her relations."

"I never thought he would get over it, I must say," said Peter Ivanovich aloud; "it is a great pity."

"What was really the matter with him?"

"The doctors can't exactly decide. Or, rather, they have decided, but all their opinions differ. When I saw him last it seemed to me that he was getting better."

"So I thought, and I have not seen him for some time. He was quite collected."

"What were his circumstances?"

"It appears his wife has precious little. There's some trifle, I believe."

"One ought to call. They live a frightful distance off."

"Far away from you, no doubt, very far."

"Well, you cannot expect me to live in the suburbs," said Peter Ivanovich, smiling at Shebek. And they began talking of how great the distances were in the city, and then resumed the session.

Independently of the potential permutations and transfers likely to result in official circles from this death, the mere fact of the death itself of a close acquaintance excited, as usual, in all who heard it, a feeling of satisfaction that the hearers survived.

"Ah! he has died, and here am I alive," was what everyone thought or felt. Moreover, the close acquaintances, including the so-called friends of Ivan Il'ich, on this occasion involuntarily reflected that now they would have to fulfil the very tiresome obligations of propriety, and attend the Panikhida besides waiting upon the widow with their condolences.

The nearest neighbours were Theodor Vasilevich and Peter Ivanovich.

Peter Ivanovich was a member of the College of Jurisprudence, and considered himself under obligations to Ivan Il'ich.

After communicating to his wife at dinner the news of the death of Ivan Il'ich, and of the idea and the possibility of transferring his own brother-in-law into their circle, Ivan Ivanovich sighed sincerely, put on his frock-coat, and went to the house of Ivan Il'ich.

At the entrance to the quarters of Ivan Il'ich stood a carriage and two coachmen. Below, in the antechamber, near the coatstand, leaning against the wall, was the glazed lid of the coffin, adorned with tassels and galloon, and furbished up with powder to look like new. Two ladies in black were taking off their furs. One was the sister of Ivan Il'ich, whom he knew, the other was a stranger. Peter Ivanovich's colleague, Schwarz, was coming downstairs, and from the top step saw the new arrival; he stopped short, and winked at him, as much as to say: "Ivan Il'ich has made a mess of it; what have we got to do with it?"

Schwarz's face, with its English whiskers, and his long, lean figure in its frock-coat, had, as usual, an air of refined solemnity, and this solemnity, always diametrically opposed to the humorous character of Schwarz, had here a peculiar piquancy. So, at any rate, thought Peter Ivanovich.

Peter Ivanovich let the ladies go on before him, and slowly ascended the staircase behind them. Schwarz did not descend, but remained at the top. Peter Ivanovich understood why: he wanted to arrange with him where they were to meet to-day. The ladies went up the staircase to the widow, but Schwarz, with his strong lips in a serious pose, and a waggish look, indicated by a movement of the brows that the room where the corpse lay was to the right.

Peter Ivanovich, as was always the case with him, entered with a feeling of uncertainty as to what he ought to do there. One thing he was quite certain of — one should never fail to cross oneself on such occasions. As to whether it was also necessary to genuflect, he was not quite sure, so he adopted a middle course: on entering the room he proceeded to cross himself, and just made a slight pretence of genuflecting. As much as this pantomime with his hands and head allowed him to do so, he glanced round the room. Two young men, one of them a gymnasiast, both apparently relatives, were coming out of the room, crossing themselves. An old woman was standing there immovably, and a lady, with pointedly arched brows, was saying something to her in a whisper. A d'yachek in a cassock, alert and emphatic, was reading something aloud, with an expression excluding all contradiction; the muzhik-waiter, Gerasim, passing in front of Peter Ivanovich with light steps, was strewing something on the floor. No sooner had he noticed this than Peter Ivanovich was sensible of the faint odour of a corpse. Last time he had called upon Ivan Il'ich, Peter Ivanovich had seen this muzhik in the cabinet; he served as a nurse, and Ivan Il'ich was particularly fond of him. Peter Ivanovich kept on crossing him- self, and slightly genuflecting in a central position, between the coffin, the d'yachek, and the images on the wall in the corner. Presently, when this action of crossing himself seemed to him to have lasted quite long enough, he stopped short, and began to look at the corpse. The corpse lay particularly heavily, as is the way with corpses, its stark-cold members sinking inwardly towards the bottom of the coffin, with the head projecting somewhat from the pillow, and prominently exhibited, as corpses always do exhibit, its yellow waxen forehead with the bald patches on the emaciated temples, and the prominent nose almost embedded in the upper lip. He had changed very much. He was even thinner than when Peter Ivanovich had last seen him; but, as is the case with all corpses, the face had become handsomer, more distinguished looking, than it had been in life — that was the most noticeable change. On the face there was an expression which said that what it was necessary to do had been done, and done rightly. Moreover, in the expression of the face there was something besides, either a reproach or a recollection, of something in life. This recollection seemed to Peter Ivanovich incongruous, or, at least, inapplicable to him. He had an unpleasant sort of feeling, and therefore Peter Ivanovich hastily crossed himself once more, and, as it seemed to him, much too hastily and incompatibly with decent observance, and he turned and went towards the door. Schwarz was awaiting him in the vestibule, with his legs stretched far apart, and drumming with both hands on the sides of his top hat One glance at the humorous, wholesome, and elegant figure of Schwarz quite refreshed Peter Ivanovich. Peter Ivanovich understood that he, Schwarz, stood high above all that, and refused to submit to depressing influences. A single glance of his said: The incident of the panikhida of Ivan Il'ich is absolutely no sufficient occasion for the interruption of the recognised order of things; in other words, nothing could interfere with the shuffling of a pack of cards that very evening, and the dealing them out, while the lackeys were putting four freshly lighted candles in their proper places; and, in general, there was no reason for supposing that this incident could prevent us from spending together a pleasant evening to-day as on all other days. He said as much to Peter Ivanovich as he passed by, and invited him to join them in a card party at Theodor Vasilevich's. But, plainly, it was not the fate of Peter Ivanovich to amuse himself that evening. Praskov'ya Thedorovna, a short, fat woman, and, despite every architectural, effort of her own in the contrary direction, expanding down-wards from the shoulders, all in black, with a lace hood, and with just the same strangely raised eyebrows as the lady standing before the coffin, came out of her apartments with other ladies, and, conducting them to the dead man's door, said:

"The panikhida will take place immediately, go in!"

Schwarz, bowing indefinitely, remained where he was, obvi-ously neither declining nor accepting this invitation. Praskov'ya Thedorovna, observing Peter Ivanovich, sighed, came straight towards him, took his hand, and said:

"I know that you were a sincere friend of Ivan Il'ich," and kept looking at him, expecting from him actions correspond-ing with these words.

Peter Ivanovich knew that just as it had been necessary to cross himself a little time ago, so now it was necessary to press the lady's hand, sigh, and say:

"Believe me, I Was indeed."

And he did so. And, having so done, he felt that the result desired was obtained — he was touched and she was touched.

"Come, before they begin in there, I want to have a little talk with you," said the widow; "give me your hand."

Peter Ivanovich gave his hand, and they proceeded together to an inner apartment, past Schwarz, who gave Peter Ivan-ovich a melancholy wink.

"It's all up with our game! Don't try and come, we'll look out for another partner," was what his waggish look said.

Peter Ivanovich sighed, still more deeply and sadly, and Praskov'ya Thedorovna gratefully pressed his arm. Entering her drawing-room, tapestried in pink cretonne, and lit by a dim shaded lamp, they sat down at the table, she on the divan, and Peter Ivanovich on a low seat with disordered springs and irregularly disposed down-stuffing, which gave way beneath him. Praskov'ya Thedorovna would have insisted on his taking another seat, but reflected that such insistence was incongruous with her situation, and thought better of it. As he sat down on the soft cushioned seat, Peter Ivanovich called to mind how Ivan Il'ich had designed the ornamentation of this room, and had consulted him about the pink cretonne with the green leaves. As she sat on the divan, after steering her way round the table (the whole drawing-room, by the way, was crowded with knick-knacks and furniture), the black lace of the widow's black dress caught in the carving of the table. Peter Ivanovich started up to unfasten it, and the downy cushion, freed from the pressure of his body, sprang up and bumped him. The widow herself stood up, and began to unfasten her lace, and Peter Ivanovich again sat down, suppressing the rebellious down-stuffing beneath him. But the widow did not quite detach herself, and Peter Ivanovich again rose up, and again the stuffing rose in rebellion and even the springs creaked. When everything was at last arranged, the lady drew forth a clean batiste pocket-handkerchief, and began to weep. But the episode of the lace and the struggle with the down cushion had somewhat cooled Peter Ivanovich, and he sat down somewhat sulkily. This awkward situation was interrupted by Sokolov, Ivan Il'ich's butler, with the announcement that the place in the churchyard which Praskov'ya Thedorovna had fixed upon would cost 200 roubles. She ceased to weep, and, with a victimised air, glanced at Peter Ivanovich, and remarked that it was a heavy price for her to pay. Peter Ivanovich made a deprecatory gesture, expressing his indubitable conviction that it could not very well be otherwise.

"Pray smoke!" she said, in a voice at once magnanimous and despondent, and she began discussing with Sokolov the question of the price of the grave.

Peter Ivanovich, as he smoked, heard how circumstantially she inquired about the prices of the different plots of ground, and fixed upon the one she ought to take. Then, having settled at last about the plot of ground, she settled about the singers. Sokolov withdrew.

"I do everything myself," she said to Peter Ivanovich, pushing aside the albums lying on the table; and observing that the tobacco ash was threatening the table, she unobtrusively insinuated an ash tray close to Peter Ivanovich, without interrupting her conversation; "I should consider it hypocritical to assert that I cannot attend to practical things for sheer grief. On the contrary, if anything can, I will not say relieve, but distract my thoughts — it is this caring for him."

Again she got ready her handkerchief, as if making up her mind to weep, and suddenly, as if doing violence to herself, she shook her head and began to speak calmly.

"However, I have business to transact with you."

Peter Ivanovich bowed, without allowing free play to the springs of his cushioned seat, which immediately grew unruly beneath him.

"He suffered terribly at the last."

"Did he suffer very much? " inquired Peter Ivanovich.

"Ah, frightfully! At the last he never ceased to cry out — not for minutes, but for hours at a time. For three days in succession he cried out without any variation of voice. It was insupportable. I can't understand how I managed to stand it; we could hear him through three doors. Alas! What have I not endured!"

"But was he really conscious?" inquired Peter Ivanovich.

"Yes," she whispered, "to the very last moment. He took leave of us a quarter of an hour before his death, and even asked us to bring Voloda to him."

The thought of the sufferings of the man he had known so intimately, first of all as a merry child and schoolfellow, and afterwards, when he had grown up, as a colleague, despite the unpleasant consciousness of his hypocrisy and the hypocrisy of this woman, suddenly terrified Peter Ivanovich. Again he saw before him that forehead, and the nose pressing upon the upper lip, and he had a feeling of horror on his own account

"Three whole days of terrible suffering — and death. The same thing may befall me, suddenly, at any moment," he thought, and for an instant he had a sensation of horror. But immediately, he himself knew not how, there came to his assistance the usual reflection that this thing had happened to Ivan Il'ich and not to him; that it ought not, and could not, happen to him, and that, by giving way to the thought of it, he was only giving way to a gloomy tendency which he ought not to give way to, as Schwarz's face had plainly declared. And having made this reflection, Peter Ivanovich felt more comfortable, and began with interest to inquire about the particulars of the end of Ivan Il'ich, as if death was an accident to which only Ivan Il'ich was liable, but he himself was not.

After various discussions about the really terrible physical sufferings endured by Ivan Il'ich (Peter Ivanovich learnt these particulars simply because the torments of Ivan Il'ich were really upon the nerves of Praskov'ya Thedorovna), the widow evidently thought it was necessary to come to the point.

"Alas! Peter Ivanovich," said she, "how hard it is, how terribly hard, how terribly hard," and she burst into tears.

Peter Ivanovich sighed, and waited for her to dry her eyes. When she had dried her eyes, he said: "Believe in my sympathy!" And again she began to talk, and told him what was evidently her real business with him: it amounted to asking him how she was to set about obtaining some money from the Treasury on the occasion of her husband's death. She pretended to be asking the advice of Peter Ivanovich as to getting a pension; but he saw that she already knew all about it down to the minutest particular — nay, knew, what he did not know, the best means of extorting everything possible from the Treasury, with her husband's death as a pretext. What she

9

really wanted to know was, whether it were possible, somehow or other, to extract still a little more money than was strictly due? Peter Ivanovich tried to devise some such expedient, but, after making some suggestions, and even, for decency's sake, cursing the Government for its niggardliness, he said that it seemed to him nothing more could be got. Then she sighed, and obviously was beginning to cast about for some means of ridding herself of her visitor. He understood this, extinguished his cigarette, pressed her hand, and went into the antechamber.

In the dining-room, with the clocks with which Ivan Il'ich had been so pleased (he bought them in a bric-à-brac shop), Peter Ivanovich met the priest and some other acquaintances coming to the panikhida, and he saw a handsome young gentlewoman whom he also knew, the daughter of Ivan Il'ich. She was all in black. Her slim figure seemed slimmer than ever. She had a gloomy, resolute, almost angry look. She bowed to Peter Ivanovich as if lie were to blame for something. Behind the daughter, with just the same aggrieved look, stood an acquaintance of Peter Ivanovich, a rich young man, employed in the Courts, her fiancé as Peter Ivanovich understood. He bowed to them with a dispirited expression, and was about to make his way into the dead man's room, when there appeared on the top of the staircase the figure of the son of the house, the gymnasiast, frightfully like Ivan Il'ich. It was Ivan Il'ich as a youth, as Peter Ivanovich remembered him when he was a law student. His eyes were all red with weeping, and just like the eyes of dirty little boys of thirteen or fourteen. The youth, on perceiving Peter Ivanovich, began to frown, half severely, half shamefacedly. Peter Ivanovich nodded to him, and proceeded into the dead man's room. The panikhida began — lights, groans, incense, tears, sobs. Peter Ivanovich stood there, with puckered brows, gazing in front of him at his feet. Not once did he look at the corpse, and to the very end did not once give way to softening influences, and was one of the first to go out. There was nobody in the antechamber. Gerasim, the butler's assistant, came running out of the room of the deceased, fumbled with his strong hands over all the pelisses in order to get at the pelisse of Peter Ivanovich, and handed it to him.

"Well, Gerasim, my friend!" said Peter Ivanovich, for the sake of saying something, "a sad affair, isn't it?"

"It is the will of God; we shall all have to go through the same thing," said Gerasim, showing his white, compact, clod-hopper teeth, and like a man in the whirl of strenuous work, he briskly opened the door, called to the coachman, helped Peter Ivanovich to his seat, and sprang back to the staircase, as if occupied by the thought of all he had still to do.

Peter Ivanovich felt a particular delight in breathing the fresh air, after the smell of the incense, the corpse, and the carbolic acid.

"Where to?" asked the coachman.

"It is not late. I'll go to Theodor Vasilevich's."

And so Peter Ivanovich went. And, in fact, he found them at the end of the first rubber, so he just came in time to take a hand.

CHAPTER II

The past history of the life of Ivan Il'ich was most simple and ordinary, and most terrible. Ivan Il'ich died in his forty-eighth year, he was an official in the Law Courts. He was the son of an official who had made his way in St. Petersburg through various Ministries and Departments, following a career which brings people into a certain position from which, although it has clearly been proved that they are unfit for any sort of real service, they cannot be discharged by reason of their long past services and the rank to which they have attained; and, therefore, they get fictitious sinecures, to which by no means fictitious thousands — from six to ten — are attached, on which they go on living to an advanced old age.

Such a man was Privy Councillor Il'ya Efimovich Golovin, a superfluous member of various superfluous institutions.

He had three sons. Ivan Il'ich was his second son. The eldest son went through the same career as his father, only in another Ministry, and was already drawing near to that period of official life which is rewarded by a lucrative sinecure. The third son was a failure. He had failed in various places, and was now employed on the railway; and his father and his brothers, and, more particularly, his brothers' wives, not only did not like to meet him, but, except when it was absolutely impossible to do so, altogether ignored his existence. Ivan Il'ich was looked upon as el phenix de la famille. He was not so cold and careful as his elder brother, but not such a desperate character as the younger. He was the happy medium — a sensible, vivacious, amiable, respectable man. He was educated for the law, along with his younger brother. The younger brother did not finish his studies, and was expelled from the fifth class, but Ivan Il'ich did well. In the law schools he was already what he was to be in the future all his life— a capable man, gay, good-natured, and sociable, but severely scrupulous in doing what he considered his duty and he considered as his duty whatever highly placed people looked upon as such. Neither as a youth, nor as a grown-up man, was he ever a place-hunter, yet there was this about him from his very earliest years: as a fly is attracted to a candle, so he was always drawn towards the highest placed people in his own particular sphere, appropriated their ways, their views of life, and established amicable relations with them. All the distractions of childhood and youth passed him by without leaving any particular trace upon him; he yielded to sensuality, to ambition, and, finally, while in the higher classes, to liberalism, but always within certain limits, which his feelings of propriety indicated to him beforehand.

It was while he was a law student that he had indulged himself in things which he had regarded as disgusting before he did them, and which filled him with self loathing at the very time when he was doing them; but, subsequently, perceiving that such things were done even by people in the highest positions, and were not considered bad, he himself did not indeed regard them as good, but simply forgot about them altogether, and never worried himself by thinking about them.

Quitting the schools of jurisprudence when he had risen to the tenth class, and receiving from his father money for his uniform, Ivan Il'ich ordered a suit from the fashionable tailor, Sharmer, hung on his watch chain a medal with the inscription, respice finem; took leave of his principals and his instructors; dined with his comrades once or twice at Dinons; and with a new modish trunk, linen, suits of clothes, toilet and shaving requisites, and a plaid, ordered and paid for at the very best shops, he set off for the provinces, to take the place of confidential clerk to the Governor which his father had obtained for him.

In the provinces Ivan Il'ich contrived to make his position as easy and pleasant as it had been in the schools of jurisprudence. He worked hard, made a career for himself, and at the same time amused himself pleasantly and respectably. Occasionally, he was despatched by the Government on tours of investigation, always observing a dignified bearing towards both high and low, always remarkable for a scrupulous and incorruptible integrity of which he could not fail to be proud, and satisfactorily accomplishing every commission entrusted to him, more especially those relating to the dissenters.

Despite his youth and a natural bias towards light gaiety, in all business relations connected with the service he was extraordinarily firm, official, and even severe; but in society he was frequently sportive and witty, and always good-humoured, gentlemanly, and bon enfant, as his chief and his chiefs wife, with whom he was always at home, used to say.

There was a liaison with one of the ladies who had been attracted to the elegant jurist in the provinces; there was also a little milliner; there were also drinking-parties with casual wing-adjutants, and excursions into a certain remote street after supper; there were also some underhand services rendered to the chief, and even to the wife of the chief; but all this was carried off with such an air of good breeding that it was impossible to give it a bad name, so it was all put down as a necessary part of the French postulate, il faut que jeunesse se passe. It was all carried on with clean hands, in clean shirts, with French words, and, the main thing, in the very highest society, consequently with the sanction of persons of the highest rank.

This was the course of Ivan Il'ich's life for five years, and then there was a change in the service. New judicial departments appeared, and new men were required to fill them.

And Ivan Il'ich became one of these new men.

The post of investigating magistrate was offered to Ivan Il'ich, and Ivan Il'ich accepted it, notwithstanding the fact that this place was in another Government, and he would have to break off his existing relations and establish new ones. Ivan Il'ich's friends showed their appreciation of him; they laid their heads together, presented him with a silver cigarette holder, and off he went to his new appointment.

As an investigating magistrate, Ivan Il'ich was just as comme il fat and gentlemanly as before, sensibly keeping his official obligations and his private life quite apart, and inspiring general respect, as became a civil, servant with a special commission. Indeed, the office of magistrate was much more interesting and attractive to Ivan Il'ich than his previous appointment. In his previous appointment it had been very pleasant in his fashionable uniform, and with a free and easy gait, to stroll past the tremulous and expectant crowd of petitioners and minor official personages awaiting an audience outside, who envied him the privilege of going straight into the chiefs private room, and sitting with him over cigarettes and tea; but there were very few people who directly depended upon his good pleasure. Such people were only the subordinate local magistrates and the dissenters who overwhelmed him with petitions, and he loved to converse with such dependent folks politely, nay, almost as a comrade; he loved to make them feel that he, who could have crushed them if he liked, preferred to treat them amicably and in quite a homely way. Then, however, there were very few of such people. But now that he was an investigating magistrate, Ivan Il'ich felt that all, all without exception, even the most important, self-satisfied people — all of them were in his hands, and that he had only to write certain words on a piece of headed paper, and the most important, self-satisfied person would instantly be brought before him, either as a criminal or a witness, and, unless he chose to ask him to sit down, would have to stand before him and answer his questions. Ivan Il'ich never abused his authority, on the contrary, he tried to soften its expression; but the consciousness of this authority, and of his power to soften it, constituted, so far as he was concerned, the principal interest and attraction of his new office. In his own department, especially in his judicial investigations, Ivan Il'ich very speedily adopted the plan of ignoring all circumstances not directly concerning the service, and of presenting even the most complicated affair in such a form as only superficially to express it on paper, at the same time completely excluding his personal views, and especially observing all the requisite formalities. This was a new way of doing things.

On being transferred to a new town, in the capacity of examining magistrate, Ivan Il'ich made fresh acquaintances, contracted fresh ties, established himself anew, and adopted a somewhat different tone. He took up a position of dignified aloofness as regards the governmental authorities, and chose a better circle from among the magistrates and rich gentry dwelling in the town, and adopted a tone of slight disapproval towards the Government — a tone of moderate liberalism and enlightened citizenship. Moreover, without making any change in the elegance of his toilet, Ivan Il'ich, in his new dignity, ceased to shave closely, and gave his beard liberty to grow as it liked.

The life of Ivan Il'ich in this new town arranged itself very pleasantly. The society in which he lived, and which was for ever skirmishing with the Governor, was good and amicable, his salary was larger, and not a little delight was added to life in those days by whist, which Ivan Il'ich now began to play, having the capacity of playing at cards gaily, with a quick eye for combinations, and with considerable finesse, so that, generally speaking, he was always on the winning side.

After two years of service in the new town, Ivan Il'ich encountered his future wife. Praskov'ya Thedorovna Mikhel was a most fascinating, sensible, brilliant girl, belonging to Ivan Il'ich's own circle. In the number of his other pastimes and relaxations from the cares of a magistrate, Ivan Il'ich included his light and sportive relations with Praskov'ya Thedorovna.

Ivan Il'ich, as a subordinate official, generally danced, as a judge he only danced on exceptional occasions. It was, as if he said: Though I have now different functions, and am in the fifth class, nevertheless, if a dance must be danced, I will show that I can do better than others even in that respect. So, now and then, he would dance of an evening with Praskov'ya Thedorovna, and it was principally during these dances that he made a conquest of Praskov'ya Thedorovna. She fell in love with him. Ivan Il'ich had no clear, fixed intention of marrying; but when the girl fell in love with him, he put himself this question: "Why, indeed, should I not marry?"

The girl, Praskov'ya Thedorovna, was of a good old family, and not bad-looking; she also had a little property of her own. Ivan Il'ich might calculate on making a much more brilliant match, yet this was not a bad match. Ivan Il'ich had his salary, and she, so he reckoned, had about the same. Her family was a good one, and she was a gentle, very pretty, and thoroughly well-principled woman. To say that Ivan Il'ich married because he was in love with his fianciè, and found in her a sympathy with his views of life, would have been as inaccurate as to say that he married because the people of his circle had approved of the match. Ivan Il'ich married for two reasons: it was pleasant to him to acquire such a wife, and, at the same time, he did what people of the highest position considered the proper thing to do.

So Ivan Il'ich married.

The very process of marriage and the first period of his wedded life, with the conjugal caresses, the new furniture, the new plate, the new linen, right up to the pregnancy of his wife, passed very well, so that Ivan Il'ich really began to think that his marriage would not interrupt that light, pleasant, merry, and always dignified mode of life approved of by society, which Ivan Il'ich regarded as his own proper life in general, but would even add to its charms. But now, during the first months of his wife's pregnancy, there came to light something so new, unexpected, unpleasant, difficult, and unbecoming, that he could not have anticipated it and never could get over it.

His wife, without any occasion for it, or so it seemed to Ivan Il'ich, and from pure de gaité de cœur, as he phrased it, began to destroy the equilibrium and dignity of his life: without the slightest cause she began to be jealous, exacted the utmost attention from him, tried to pick quarrels on all occasions, and had unpleasant and even coarse scenes with him.

At first Ivan Il'ich did his best to free himself from the unpleasantness of this situation by adopting the same easy and dignified way of treating life in general which had served him in such good stead before; he tried to ignore his wife's state of mind, and continued to live, as before, easily and pleasantly; he invited parties of friends to his house, and tried going to the club and accepting invitations himself. But his wife on one occasion abused him so coarsely and energetically, and so persistently continued so to abuse him every time he did not comply with her demands, evidently determined not to desist till he should have submitted, or in other words, should have consented to sit moping at home like herself, that Ivan Il'ich grew alarmed. He understood now that conjugal life — at any rate, conjugal life with his wife — was not always the same thing as a pleasant and dignified life; but, on the contrary, often made such a life impossible, and that, therefore, it was necessary to compensate himself for the loss of it. So Ivan Il'ich began seeking such compensation. His official position was the part of his life which impressed Praskov'ya Thedorovna the most, and Ivan Il'ich, by means of his official position and the obligations resulting therefrom, began a contest with his wife in her endeavours to limit his independent existence.

The birth of the infant, the various attempts to nourish it, the various ensuing disappointments, the illnesses, real and imaginary, of mother and child, in all of which Ivan Il'ich was supposed to sympathize, though he knew nothing at all about it — all these things made it more and more urgently necessary for Ivan Il'ich to try and form another world for himself quite outside the family circle.

Thus, in proportion as his wife became more and more irritating and exacting, Ivan Il'ich more and more transferred the centre of gravity of his existence to his official existence. He began to love his office still more, and became more ambitious than he had ever been before.

Very soon, not more than a year after his marriage, Ivan Il'ich understood that marriage, though generally regarded as one of the chief commodities of life, is in reality a very complicated and difficult affair, with regard to which, if he wished to do his duty, that is to say, lead the decent sort of life approved of by society, he must take up a definite position, as he had done in his official life.

And Ivan Il'ich succeeded in taking up such definite position in his married life. He required of his family life only those domestic commodities, eg., a dinner, a housewife, a bed, etc., which it was able to give, and, in particular, that decency of external forms which is desiderated by public opinion. For the rest he looked for cheerful amiability, and was very grateful if he found it. But whenever he encountered opposition or peevishness, he immediately went off to his separate, penned-off world of official life, where everything was pleasant.

Ivan Il'ich was valued as a good official, and in three years he was made the colleague of the procurator. Fresh obligations, their importance, the power of examining everyone before the tribunal and putting them in prison, the publicity of his speeches, the success which attended Ivan Il'ich in his new capacity — all this made the public service still more attractive to him.

Children continued to arrive. His wife grew still more cross and peevish, but the position which Ivan Il'ich had successfully assumed with regard to his domestic life made him almost invulnerable to her peevishness.

After seven years of service in one town, Ivan Il'ich was transferred to another government as procurator. They migrated thither; there was little money, and his wife did not like the place to which they had been transferred. The salary was larger, indeed, than before, but living was also dearer; moreover, two of their children died, and therefore family life became still more unpleasant to Ivan Il'ich.

Praskov'ya Thedorovna, in this new place, reproached her husband for every little mishap which happened. The greater part of the subjects of conversation between the husband and wife, especially the education of the children, led to debates bordering on quarrels, and quarrels were ready to burst forth every moment. There remained only those rare periods of reviving affection which all consorts experience from time to time, but which do not last long. These were islets on which they rested for a time, only to embark again on the sea of covert hatred, which expressed itself in a mutual alienation. This alienation might have grieved Ivan Il'ich if he had considered that it ought not to be, but by this time he had come to recognise this situation not only as normal, but as the aim of his domestic existence. For it had now become his aim to free himself more and more from these unpleasantnesses, and give them an inoffensive and decent character; and he achieved his aim by spending less and less time in his family, and when he was forced to be there, he tried to alleviate his position by the presence of strangers. Ivan Il'ich's chief comfort was that he had his official employment. In the official world the whole interest of his life was concentrated. And this interest smoothed matters for him. The consciousness of his authority, of the power he had to ruin every man he wanted to ruin, even the external dignity of his entrance into Court, and his dealings with his subordinates, his success before his superiors and his subordinates, and, the main thing, his masterly conduct of affairs, of which he was quite sensible — all this delighted him, and together with his intercourse with his colleagues, dinners, and whist, quite filled up his life. So, in general, the life of Ivan

Il'ich continued to go on, as he thought it should go on, pleasantly and becomingly.

Thus, then, he continued to live for seven years. His eldest daughter was already sixteen; one more child had died, and there remained a little boy, a gymnasiast, the object of discord. Ivan Il'ich wanted to devote him to jurisprudence, and Praskov'ya Thedorovna, to spite him, sent him to the gymnasium. The daughter was educated at home, and promised well; the lad also did not do amiss with his studies.

CHAPTER III

Thus proceeded the life of Ivan Il'ich for the space of seventeen years from the time of his marriage. He was already an old procurator who had rejected several offers, because he was expecting a more desirable post, when unexpectedly something disagreeable happened which completely ruined his tranquil existence. Ivan Il'ich was expecting the post of chief assessor in a university town, but a Mr. Goppe had been too quick for him, and got the place instead. Ivan Il'ich was very angry; he began to make reproaches, and quarrel with him and with his immediate superiors; a coldness sprang up between them, and at the next vacancy he was again passed over.

This was in the year 1880. This particular year was a very heavy one in the life of Ivan Il'ich. In this year, it appeared, on the one hand, that his salary was not sufficient to live upon; and, on the other hand, everyone seemed to ignore him, and, greatest, most cruel injustice of all from his point of view, his situation seemed to others to be quite what it ought to be. Even his father considered himself under no obligation to assist him. He had a feeling that they were all deserting him, considering his position, with a salary of 3,500 roubles, quite normal, and even a lucky one. He alone knew, what with the injustice that was being done him, and with the eternal jarrings of his wife, and with the debts he was beginning to make, living, as he did, beyond his means — he alone knew that his position was far from normal.

In the summer of this year, in order to economize, he took leave of absence, and went to spend the summer with his wife in the country at the house of Praskov'ya Thedorovna's brother.

Out of service in the country, Ivan Il'ich, for the first time in his life, experienced not merely ennui, but an unendurable depression, and arrived at the conclusion that to live like this was impossible, and that it was indispensable for him to adopt some decisive measure at once.

After passing a sleepless night, the whole of which Ivan Il'ich spent on the terrace, he resolved to go to St. Petersburg, and try to get transferred into another Ministry, in order to punish those persons who did not appreciate him.

On the following day, despite all the remonstrances of his wife and brother-in-law, he went to St. Petersburg.

He went for one special purpose: to solicit a post with a salary of 5,000 roubles. He was not particular about the Ministry, or its tendencies, or the sort of work required from him. All he wanted was the post — a post worth 5,000 roubles, either in the Administrative Services, or in a bank, or a railway, or in connection with the charitable institutions of the Empress Mary, or even in the Customs — but the 5,000 salary was indispensable, and he was unalterably resolved to quit the Ministry where they did not appreciate him.

And behold! this excursion of Ivan Il'ich was crowned by amazing, unlooked-for success. In Kursk, Th. S. Ilin, an acquaintance of Ivan Il'ich, was promoted to the first class, and he communicated by telegram to the Governor of Kursk that a series of changes was impending just then in the Ministry to which he belonged, Ivan Semenovich succeeding to the post of Peter Ivanovich.

The projected change, besides its importance for Russia, had a particular significance for Ivan Il'ich, inasmuch as the newly promoted personage, Peter Petrovich, and evidently his friend, Zakhar Ivanovich, were in the highest degree favourable to Ivan Il'ich, and Zakhar Ivanovich was, moreover, a friend and colleague of Ivan Il'ich.

In Moscow the report was confirmed, and on arriving at St. Petersburg Ivan Il'ich met Zakhar Ivanovich, and received the promise of a safe place in his former Ministry, the Ministry of Justice.

In a week he telegraphed to his wife:

"Zakhar post of Miller on first announcement I receive the nomination."

Ivan Il'ich, thanks to this change of persons, unexpectedly received in his former Ministry such an important place that he stood two degrees higher than his colleagues: a salary of 5,000, and travelling fees to the amount of 3,000 more. All his rage against his former enemies and against the whole Ministry was forgotten, and Ivan Il'ich was completely happy.

Ivan Il'ich returned to the country more cheerful and contented than he had been for a long time. Praskov'ya Thedorovna was also pleased, and a truce was concluded between them. Ivan Il'ich had a lot to tell about the respect with which he had been treated at St. Petersburg, and how all they who had been his enemies had been humbled and now crouched before him ; how he was envied his new position, and especially how very much they all loved him at St. Petersburg.

Praskov'ya Thedorovna listened to all this, and made as if she believed it, and did not contradict him in anything, but was busy all the time making her own plans about the new style of life they should live in the city to which they had thus been transferred; and Ivan Il'ich perceived with joy that these plans were his plans, that they agreed together, and that his thwarted life had reacquired a bright and genuine pleasantness and dignity corresponding with his wishes.

Ivan Il'ich arrived in the capital very shortly. He had to assume his new office on September 10th, and besides that he required a little time to settle in his new home, to remove all his things from the country, to buy things that were wanted, and see to a good many other things; in a word, to establish himself as he had already made up his mind to do, and as Praskhov'ya Tedorovna had resolved to do likewise.

And now when everything had been arranged so comfortably, and when he and his wife had once more but one common object before them, and, despite the fact that they lived very little together, harmonised more amicably than they had ever done since the first year of their marriage, Ivan Il'ich thought of removing his family at once; but his sister and brother-in-law, who had suddenly become particularly friendly and kinsmanlike towards Ivan Il'ich, would not hear of it, so Ivan Il'ich had to depart by himself.

Ivan Il'ich departed then, and the happy frame of mind produced by his success and his harmonious relations with his wife, each stimulating the other, never quitted him the whole time. He hit upon excellent quarters, the sort of dwelling he and his wife had long been dreaming about. Lofty, spacious reception rooms in the old style, a convenient grandiose cabinet, rooms for his wife and daughter, a class room for his son — as if expressly designed for them. Ivan Il'ich himself undertook all the arrangements, selected the carpets, bought the furniture — old-fashioned furniture in particular, which (he took care of that) was in a particularly comme il faut style — and the coverings of the furniture, and it all grew and grew into the ideal which he had set his mind on attaining. When half his arrangements were completed, the general effect far exceeded his expectations. It presented that comme il faut, elegant, and uncommon character which satisfies every requisite when it is finished. In his slumbers he pictured to himself the drawing-room as it was going to be. Looking at the reception room, still incomplete, he already beheld the chimneypiece, the ecran, the etagère, those little chairs scattered about the room, those plates and plaques on the walls, and the bronzes when they should all be in their places. The thought pleased him how he would surprise Pasha and Lizan'ka, both of whom had taste in these matters. They never expected anything like this. He had, in particular, succeeded in discovering and buying cheap old things which gave to everything a particularly distinguished character. In his letters he purposely described everything as worse than it really was, in order to surprise them the more. All this occupied him so much that even his new post, much as he loved it, interested him far less than he had anticipated. At the sessions he attended he frequently had fits of absent-mindedness; he was thinking all the time whether the curtain-cornices were plain or ornamental. He was so taken up with this thought that he frequently took the trouble to rearrange the furniture and hang the curtains over again. Once, when he had mounted a ladder to show the unintelligent curtain-hanger how he wished the curtains draped, he stumbled and fell, but being vigorous and alert he managed to keep his feet, simply knocking his side against the handle of a frame. The bruise hurt him a little, but the pain soon passed off. All this time, indeed, Ivan Il'ich felt particularly bright and well. He wrote: "I feel that fifteen of my years have leaped from off my shoulders." He thought he should have finished in September, but the business dragged on till the middle of October. By way of compensation, it was also most excellent; it was not only he that said it, everyone who saw it told him that it was so.

In reality, it was the same with him as it is with all not very rich people who wish to imitate the rich, and, as a matter of fact, only imitate one another: silk stuffs, black wood, flowers, carpets, and bronzes, dark and shining, all that sort of thing which all persons of a certain class do in order to resemble all other persons of the same class. And with him, too, it was all so much alike that there was absolutely nothing to attract attention, yet to him it all seemed something especial. When he met his family at the railway station, he conducted them to his illuminated, ready prepared quarters, and a lackey in a white choker opened the door leading into the flower-bedizened vestibule, and then they proceeded into the reception room and the cabinet, and ah'd and oh'd with satisfaction; and he felt very happy, and guided them everywhere, imbibed their praises, and was radiant with satisfaction. That same evening, after tea, Praskov'ya Thedorovna asked him, among other things, how he had come to fall, and he laughed and explained by pantomime how he had come flying through the air, and had frightened the curtain-hanger.

"I have not been a gymnast for nothing, anyone else would have been killed, and I merely struck myself here; if you touch it it pains, but it is passing away already, it is a simple bruise."

And they began to live in their new dwelling in which, as always happens when one has had time to turn round in a new house, they discovered that all they now really wanted was one more room, and if they only had more means — for, as usual, they now discovered that their income was short of a trifle of some 500 roubles — everything would be very well indeed. Especially pleasant was the first period of their residence in the new house, when everything was not quite complete, and a finishing touch had to be added or something had to be bought, or ordered, or re-arranged, or set to rights. And although there were some disagreements between husband and wife, both of them were so contented, and there was so much to be done, that the difference was always adjusted without any great quarrel. When, however, there was nothing more to be done, things began to be a little dull, and one or two little wants were felt, but by this time acquaintances were made, habits were formed, and life was full of its occupations.

Ivan Il'ich, after spending the morning in Court, would return to dinner, and at first his spirits were good, though he suffered a little from the worries of a new domicile. Every spot on the table-cloth, on the silk stuffs, a ragged tassle in the curtains — all these little things irritated him. He had spent so much labour on his household arrangements that every derangement of them was painful to him. Yet, on the whole, the life of Ivan Il'ich passed as, according to his belief, life ought to pass — easily, gaily, becomingly. He rose at nine, drank his coffee, read his "Gazette," put on his demi-uniform, and went to Court. Here was piled up the harness in which he worked, and he readily adjusted himself to it. Petitioners, interrogatories in Court, the Court itself, sessions — public and administrative. In dealing with all this business, one had to know how to exclude everything crude — everything relating to life in the concrete — things which always impede the regular course of official affairs. It was necessary to guard against entering into anything but strictly official relations with people, and official relations had to be the one occasion for any dealings with them at all, and the relations themselves could be only official. For instance, a man might come and desire to be informed about something. Ivan Il'ich could have no relations with such an individual except in his official capacity; but if his relations with this man were official, and the terms of them were such as could be expressed on headed official paper, then within the limits of such official relations Ivan Il'ich would do all in his power for the man, and do it most emphatically, and at the same time observe the form of humane and friendly intercourse in the shape of politeness. Every cessation of intercourse carried with it the cessation of every other sort of inter-course. The capacity of isolating the official side of his charac-ter, so that it never interfered with his real life, was possessed by Ivan Il'ich in the highest degree, and long practice, com-bined with talent, enabled him to carry it out to such a degree that sometimes he even permitted himself, as a virtuoso, and by way of jest, to intermingle his human and his official rela-tions. He indulged himself this way because he felt within himself the power, whenever he pleased, to make himself purely official again, and reject the human element Ivan Il'ich managed this not only easily, pleasantly, and becomingly, but even artistically. In the intervals of business he smoked, drank tea, talked a little about politics, a little about affairs in general, a little about cards, and more than all about official nomina-tions. And wearied, but with the feeling of a virtuoso playing his part — first violin in the orchestra — to perfection, he would then return home. At home he would find, perhaps, that his wife and daughter had gone out somewhere, or they had visitors; his son was at the gymnasium or preparing his lessons with his tutor, and getting up what is usually taught at gymnasiums. It was all very good. After dinner, if there were no guests, Ivan Il'ich would read a book which might happen to be much talked about, and in the evening would settle down to business, that is to say, would read papers, refer to the statutes, compare statements, and put them under their proper rubrics. This occupation neither bored nor amused him. If he felt bored it was possible to play at vint, but if there was no vint, business was always preferable to sitting alone with his wife with nothing to do. Ivan Il'ich's chief delights were the little dinners to which he invited men and women of high position in the world, and the intercourse he then had with such persons, though as for them it was what they were used to every day, for Ivan Il'ich's drawing-room was just like any other drawing-room.

On one occasion they even had an evening party with dancing. And Ivan Il'ich was very happy, and everything went off very well, except for a great quarrel with his wife about the pastry and sweets. Praskov'ya Thedorovna had her own plans, but Ivan Il'ich insisted upon getting everything from a good pastry cook, and ordered a lot of pastry, and the quarrel arose because a lot of tarts remained over, and the pastry cook's account came to forty-five roubles. The quarrel was a big quarrel, and very unpleasant, because Praskov'ya Thedorovna said: "You're a silly fool." And he clutched hold of his head, and at the bottom of his heart he seriously thought for a moment or two of a separation. But the evening itself was a happy one. The best society was present, and Ivan Il'ich danced with the Princess Trufinova, the sister of the foundress of the celebrated charitable institution: "Take thou away my grief." His official delights were the delights of pride, his official delights were the delights of vanity, but the real joys of Ivan Il'ich were the joys of playing at vint. He confessed that after all, and despite whatever unpleasantness there might be in his life, the joy which like a light burned before all others was to sit down with good players and amiable partners at vint, four-handed, vint of course (five-handed vint did not do nearly so well, though Ivan Il'ich pretended that he loved that too), and to play a sensible, serious game (when you had a good hand), and then to have supper and drink a glass of wine. And when he went to bed after vint, especially when he had won a little (it was unpleasant to win a good deal), Ivan Il'ich would lie down to sleep in particularly good spirits.

Thus they lived. The very best circle formed around them, and important people and young people were among their visitors.

As regards the circle of their acquaintances, husband, wife, and daughter were quite agreed, and by tacit consent they shook off and rid themselves of all former various acquaintances and kinsfolks — the rabble, so to speak, who, along with the new people, flitted about the drawing-room with the new Japanese plaques on the walls. Very soon the second-rate friends ceased altogether to flit about their drawing-room, and only the very best people frequented the house of the Golivins. Young people came courting little Lizanka, and Petrishchev, the son of Dmitry Ivanovich Petrishchev, the judge, and his sole heir, began to pay attention to Liza, so that Ivan Il'ich already began to consult Praskov'ya Thedorovna as to whether they should let them go out driving together in a troika, or make a scene? Thus they continued to live. And everything went on as if it would ever be so, and everything was very good.

C H A P T E R   I V

They were all well. Ivan Il'ich sometimes said indeed that he had a bad taste in his mouth, and something was not quite right, but one could hardly call that illness.

But this little indisposition happened to increase, and passed, not yet into downright illness, but into a feeling of constant oppression in the side, accompanied by lowness of spirits. This lowness of spirits kept on increasing and increasing, and began to destroy that easy, pleasant, and decorous manner of life which had become an institution in the family of the Golivins. The husband and wife began to wrangle more and more frequently, and soon all ease and pleasantness fell away from them, and decorum alone remained, and that was only preserved with the greatest difficulty. Scenes again became more and more frequent between them, and at last there were only rare occasions when the husband and wife could meet together without an open rupture. And Praskov'ya Thedorovna said, and now not without reason, that her husband was very difficult to get on with. With her customary habit of exaggeration, she maintained that he had always had a frightful temper, and that it was only her good nature that had enabled her to put up with it for these twenty years. It was true that now, at any rate, he was the first to begin to quarrel. His peevishness always began before dinner, and often, and especially just when he had begun to eat, after the soup, for instance. He would then remark that this dish or that was spoilt, and did not taste as it ought to taste, or his son would put his elbows on the table, or his daughter's hair was untidy. And he blamed Praskov'ya Thedorovna for everything. At first, Praskov'ya Thedorovna was offended, and said unpleasant things to him, but once or twice at the beginning of dinner he had flown into such a rage that she understood that this was a morbid condition which expressed itself in him whenever he partook of food, so she calmed herself, ceased to be irritated, and merely hastened to finish the meal as soon as possible. Praskov'ya Thedorovna made a very great merit of her meekness. Having arrived at the conclusion that her husband had a frightful temper, and was making her life wretched, she began to pity herself. And the more she pitied herself, the more she hated her husband. She began to wish that he would die, but she could not wish this because then there would be no salary. And this irritated her still more against him. She accounted herself dreadfully miserable, principally because even his death would be no deliverance for her, and it irritated her to conceal this feeling, and this hidden irritation still further increased her irritation at him.

After one of these scenes, in which Ivan Il'ich had been particularly unjust, and after which he said, by way of explanation, that he had certainly been irritable, but that it was because he did not feel well, she said to him that if he were ill he ought to be cured, and insisted that he should go and see a famous doctor.

He went. Everything turned out just as he had expected, everything was as it always is. And the expectation and the intrinsic importance of the doctor, an acquaintance of his, was the same sort of thing which he knew by experience in the Courts, and the tapping and the auscultations, and the questions, demanding foregone and obviously unnecessary answers, and the doctor's look of importance, suggesting: Look here, my dear sir, you just rely upon us, and we'll put everything to rights; we know all about it, and will undoubtedly put everything to rights in one and the same way for everybody you like, no matter who he is — the whole process was just the same as it was in the Law Courts. Just as he in the Law Courts put on an impressive air with his subordinates, so also did the famous doctor put on an impressive air with him.

The doctor said: "So and so and so and so proves that so and so and so and so is the matter with your inside, but if this is not confirmed by the examination of so and so and so, then it is necessary to assume so and so and so and so. If, then, we assume so and so and so and so, then of course" — and so on and so on. So far as Ivan Il'ich was concerned, only a single question was of any importance: "Is my condition dangerous or not?" But the doctor altogether ignored this inconvenient question. From the doctor's point of view, this question was a silly one, and not under consideration; the balancing of contingencies was all that existed for him — kidney complaint, chronic catarrh, and diseases of the lower gut, for instance. It was no question of the life of Ivan Il'ich, but it was a dispute as between the kidneys and the intestines. And this dispute the doctor, in the most brilliant fashion, before Ivan Il'ich's very eyes, decided in favour of the intestines, at the same time making a reservation to the effect that an examination of his urine might furnish fresh indications, and that then the affair would be thoroughly investigated. All this was to an iota exactly the same sort of thing that Ivan Il'ich himself had done thousands of times in the same brilliant manner when he had had to do with persons before the Court. The doctor made his resumé just as brilliantly, and triumphantly, nay, even gaily regarded the doomed man over his spectacles. From the doctor's resumé Ivan Il'ich drew the conclusion that he was in a bad way, and that to the doctor, alas! and to everyone else it was all one, but that he, Ivan Il'ich, was certainly in a bad way. And this inference morbidly affected Ivan Il'ich, exciting within him a feeling of great pity for himself, and of great anger against the doctor who could be so indifferent in such an important question.

But he said nothing, but got up, laid his money on the table, and remarked with a sigh: "We sick people, no doubt, often ask you doctors untimely questions, but tell me now, plainly, is this illness dangerous or not ?"

The doctor regarded him severely with one eye through his spectacles, as if he would say: Prisoner at the bar, if you do not keep within the strict limits of regularly prescribed questions, I shall be obliged to take measures for your removal from the Court.

"I have already told you what I considered necessary and befitting," said the doctor. "An examination will show us anything further." And the doctor bowed.

Ivan Il'ich left the house slowly, sat down wearily in his sledge, and went home. All the way there he never ceased pondering over what the doctor had said, trying to translate all those involved, obscure, scientific sentences into simple language, and read into them an answer to the question: Am I in a bad way — a very bad way — or is it nothing after all? And it seemed to him that the meaning of all that the doctor had said was that he was in a bad way. Everything in the streets struck Ivan Il'ich as miserable. The coachmen were miserable, the houses were miserable, the passengers and the

33

shops were miserable. This pain — this dull, dumb pain, never ceasing for an instant, seemed, taken in connection with the enigmatical words of the doctor, to have acquired a fresh and far more serious significance. And Ivan Il'ich now listened to it with a new and heavy feeling.

He got home, and told his wife all about it. His wife listened, but in the middle of their conversation his daughter came in with her hat on; she had arranged to go out with her mother. With an effort she prevailed upon herself to sit down and listen to this tiresome affair, but did not stay long, and her mother even did not hear it to the end.

"Well, I'm very glad," said his wife, "that now you will take medicine regularly. Give me the prescription, I'll send Gerasim to the chemist" And she went away to dress.

He scarce breathed so long as she was there, but when she went out he drew a deep sigh.

"Well," said he to himself, "possibly it's nothing yet, after all."

He began to take the medicine, and followed the directions of the doctor, which were modified in consequence of the examination of the urine. But, on one occasion, it so happened that during this examination, and in what ought to have been the course of procedure after it, some blunder, some confusion took place. It was impossible to get at the doctor, and it turned out that something had been done which the doctor hadn't ordered. Either he had forgotten, or lied, or hidden something from him.

Nevertheless, Ivan Il'ich continued to follow the doctor's prescriptions all the same, and in so doing found for a time some relief.

The principal occupation of Ivan Il'ich, ever since his visit to the doctor, was the exact observance of the doctor's prescriptions as regards hygiene, the taking of drugs, and close attention to his malady and the whole mechanism of his organism.

The chief interests of Ivan Il'ich were people's diseases and people's healths. When they spoke about illnesses in his presence, or of people who were dying, or of wonderful cures, or especially of the disease from which he was suffering, he, trying all the time to conceal his emotion, listened eagerly, asked questions, and applied the answers he got to his own case.

His pain did not diminish, but Ivan Il'ich did violence to his own convictions in order to persuade himself that he was better. And he was able to deceive himself so long as nothing excited him. But no sooner did he have any unpleasantness with his wife, or any official bother, or bad cards at vint, then immediately he felt the full force of his illness. Formerly, he had put up with these little mishaps, and struggled against them, waiting for things to right themselves, and for better luck; but now every contretemps floored him, and drove him to utter despair. He would say to himself: "Look there, now! no sooner do I feel a little better, no sooner does the medicine begin to have a good effect, than this cursed misadventure or unpleasantness comes along and spoils everything. . . ." And he was furious at the misadventure, or at the people who caused him unpleasantness, and threw him back again; and he felt how these bursts of passion took it out of him, but he could not restrain himself. It would seem as if it ought to have been quite clear to him that this exasperation with circumstances and people could only increase his illness, and, therefore, he ought not to pay any attention to disagreeable circumstances, yet he came to the diametrically opposite conclusion: he said to himself that he needed quiet, and was furious at everything which disturbed this quiet, and flew into a passion at the very slightest interference. His condition grew even worse when he took to reading medical books and consulting the doctor; but this growing worse was so gradual that he was able to deceive himself by comparing one day with another, so slight was the difference from day to day. But, whenever he consulted the doctor, it seemed to him that he was going from bad to worse, and pretty rapidly, too; yet, notwithstanding this, he consulted the doctor continually.

This month he visited another medical celebrity. The second celebrity said almost the same thing as the first celebrity, only he put the same questions in a different way. And the consultation with this celebrity only increased the doubt and fear of Ivan Il'ich. A friend of a friend of his — a very good doctor — diagnosed his malady quite differently, and notwithstanding that he promised a cure, still further confused Ivan Il'ich with his questions and directions, besides confirming his doubts. A homoeopathist diagnosed the malady differently from any of the others, and gave him special medicines, which Ivan Il'ich, in profound secrecy, took for a week. And after a week, not feeling any relief, and losing confidence both in his former drugs and in his new ones, he fell into a still more woeful condition. Once a distinguished lady told him about cures effected by means of ikons. Ivan Il'ich caught himself listening intently, and believing in the story as an actual fact The incident alarmed him. "Is it possible that my intellect is failing me?" he asked himself. "Rubbish! nonsense! I must not give way to fancies, but must choose one doctor, and regularly follow his prescriptions. I'll do so, and there's an end of it. I'll think no more about it, but will take his drugs for a whole year. And then we shall see. And now I have done with all this vacillation!" It was easy to say this, but impossible to accomplish it. All along, the pain in his side was tormenting him, and, as if growing in strength, it began to be more insistent; the taste in his mouth became stronger, it seemed to him as if a disgusting smell proceeded from the inside of his mouth, and his appetite and strength failed him more and more. It was impossible to deceive himself any longer: something strange, novel, and so important, that nothing of anything like the same importance had ever happened in Ivan Il'ich's life before, was accomplishing itself within him. And he alone knew of it; all those around him did not or would not understand it, and thought that everything in the world was going on just the same as before. This tortured Ivan Il'ich almost more than anything else. The people at home, principally his wife and daughter, who were in the very thick of their social engagements, did not understand it at all, he could see that, and were quite offended with him for being so glum and exacting, as if he were to be blamed for that. Although they tried to hide it, he could see that he was in their way, but that his wife had forced herself to take up a certain attitude with regard to his complaint, and adhered to it, independently of whatever he might say or do. This attitude of hers was something of this sort: "You know," she would say to her acquaintances, "Ivan Il'ich cannot, like all other good people, strictly adhere to the doctor's prescriptions. To-day he takes his drops and eats what he is ordered to eat, and will lie down a bit; and then to-morrow, if I don't look after him, he will forget to take them; he will eat sturgeon (which is forbidden him), and will sit down to cards for a whole hour."

"When did I?" Ivan Il'ich said angrily at Peter Ivanovich's.

"In the evening with Shebek."

"What does it matter? I cannot sleep for pain."

"Very well; whatever may be done, you will never be cured, and you'll keep on giving us all this anxiety."

This extraneous attitude of Praskov'ya Thedorovna towards the sick man, as expressed to others and to himself, implied that the illness was all Ivan Il'ich's own fault, and was, in fact, a fresh unpleasantness which he was causing his wife. Ivan Il'ich felt indeed that this escaped her involuntarily, but it was none the easier to bear for all that

In the Courts, too, Ivan Il'ich observed, or thought he observed, the same strange sort of attitude taken up towards him. At one time it would seem to him as if they regarded him as a man whose place would soon be vacant; then all at once his friends would begin to joke with him about his faddiness, just as if that strange and terrible, unheard of thing that was going on within him, never ceasing to suck away at him, and irresistibly dragging him somewhither, was the most pleasant subject in the world for jesting. Schwarz especially irritated him by his sportiveness, vivacity, and comme il faut way of looking at things, reminding Ivan Il'ich of what he was himself ten years ago.

A party of friends would come and sit down with him to a game at cards, in the lightest, merriest of moods, and the cards would be sorted and dealt, and the usual jests would circulate, and suddenly Ivan Il'ich would be sensible of his sucking pain and of that bad taste in the mouth, and it would seem a barbarous thing to him that he could take any pleasure in the game under such circumstances.

They could all see how hard it was for him, and they would say to him: "We can stop if you are tired. You rest a bit."

Rest a bit? No, he could not think of resting; he would play the rubber.

They were all glum and silent, and Ivan Il'ich felt that he had cast this glumness upon them, and could not dissipate it. Then they had supper and separated, and Ivan Il'ich was left all alone with the consciousness that his life was envenomed, and that he was envenoming the lives of others, and that this venom would not lose in intensity, but would go on penetrating his existence more and more.

And with the consciousness of this, and what is more, with acute physical pain and even with terror, he was obliged to lie down on his bed, unable to sleep for great pain the whole night And in the morning he had to get up, dress himself, go to Court, speak, write, and if he did not go he had to remain for four-and-twenty hours at home, each one of which was a

torment. And he had thus to go on living on the brink of destruction, without a single soul to understand and pity him.

C H A P T E R   V

And thus a month, two months, passed away. Just before
the new year his brother-in-law came to town, and stayed with
them. Ivan Il'ich was at Court. Praskov'ya Thedorovna had
gone out shopping. On entering his cabinet he found his
brother-in-law there, a healthy fellow of sanguine tempera-
ment, unpacking his own trunk. He raised his head on hearing
the footsteps of Ivan Il'ich, and glanced at him for a moment in
silence. This look revealed everything to Ivan Il'ich. His brother-in-law opened his mouth to sigh, and restrained himself.
This movement confirmed everything.

"Well, I've altered a bit, eh?"

"Yes . . . there's a change."

And however much Ivan Il'ich might try to bring his brother-in-law to converse on the subject of his appearance, his
brother-in-law continued to be reticent Praskov'ya Thedorovna arrived, and the brother-in-law went to her. Ivan
Il'ich locked the door and began to look at himself in the mirror — full-face first of all, and after that sideways. He took up
his portrait, in which he was represented with his wife, and
compared the portrait with what he saw in the glass. The
change was enormous. Then he stripped up his shirt-sleeve to
the elbow, regarded it, let down his sleeve again, sat down on
the ottoman, and grew blacker than night.

"It must not be, it must not be," he said to himself, sprang
up, went to the table, opened some public document, began to
read it, but could not go on with it. He opened the door and

went into the saloon. The door leading to the drawing-room was closed. He approached it on tip-toe and began to listen.

"No, you exaggerate," Praskov'ya Thedorovna was saying.

"Exaggerate? Why, surely you can see for yourself ? He's a dead man, I tell you; look at his eyes! No light in 'em. What's the matter with him?"

"Nobody knows. Nikolaev (this was the friendly doctor) said something or other, but I don't know what to make of it. Leshchetetsky (this was the former doctor) said on the other hand . . ."

Ivan Il'ich went away, went to his own room, lay down, and began to think: "Reins, renal flux," He remembered all that the doctors had told him, how his renal mischief had begun, and how it was spreading now here and now there. And by the force of the imagination he tried to understand this malady, and how to stop it and cure it. Such a very little was wanted, it seemed to him. " No, I will go again to Peter Ivanovich." (This was the friend whose friend the doctor was.) He rang, ordered them to get the carriage ready, and prepared to go.

"Where are you going, Jean?" asked his wife, with a peculiarly melancholy, and unusually kind expression.

This unusually kind expression offended him. He regarded her gloomily.

"I must go to Peter Ivanovich."

He went to this friend whose friend the doctor was, and with him he went to the doctor. He found him in and had a long talk with him.

After considering all the anatomical and physiological details which, according to the opinion of the doctor, accounted for what was going on inside him, he understood everything.

There was a patch — a tiny little patch in the lower gut. All that could be put to rights. The energy of one organ could be strengthened by diminishing the activity of another organ; healthy processes could be set going, and all would be made right He was a little late for dinner. He had a little dinner, talked gaily, but for a long time could not settle down to any occupation. At last he went to his cabinet and immediately set to work. He read cases and worked away, but the consciousness that there was gnawing away at him a postponed, serious, suppressed something with which he would finally have to do, never once left him. When he had finished his work he recollected that this suppressed thing was the thought of the lower gut But he did not give way to it, he went to the drawing-room for some tea. Guests were there, and there was conversation, and music, and singing, and the judge whom they wished to be his daughter's fiancé was present. Ivan Il'ich spent the evening, Praskov'ya Thedorovna observed, more gaily than the others, but not for a moment did he forget the weighty, postponed thought of the lower gut. At eleven o'clock he took leave of his guests, and went to his own room. Ever since the beginning of his illness he had slept alone in a little apartment off his cabinet. There he went, undressed, and took up a romance of Zola's, but instead of reading it fell a-thinking. And in his imagination the much-desired improvement of the small gut was accomplished. There was re-absorption, suppuration, and the proper functional activity was restored "That's the whole thing," he said to himself; "all you've got to do is to assist nature." He remembered that he had to take his medicine, got up, took it, lay down on his back, waiting for the beneficial action of the medicine to destroy the pain. "All one has to do is to take things calmly and avoid prejudicial influences, and now, indeed, I really feel better, very much better." He began to feel his side, and the contact was not painful. "Yes, I do not feel it; really I am very much better already." He put out the light and lay down on his side. The small gut evidently was righting, readjusting itself. Suddenly he felt the familiar, old, dragging pain, the same obstinate, steady, serious pain. And in his mouth there was the same fa-

miliar foulness. His heart began to throb and his head to grow
dull. "My God! my God!" he exclaimed, "again, again, and it
never ceases." And suddenly the thing struck him from a new
point of view. "Lower gut! inflammation indeed!" he said to
himself. "It is no question of the intestines, it is no question of
inflammation — it is a question of life and death. Yes, it used
to be life, and now it is drifting away, drifting away, and I can-
't stop it. Yes. Why deceive myself? Is it not quite plain to
everyone but myself that I am dying, and it is only a question
of weeks, of days— it may happen any moment? It was light,
and now it is darkness. Then I was there, and now I am here.
Where?" A cold shiver came over him — he stopped breathing. He heard only the beating of his heart

"I shall be no more, what does it mean? There will be nothing at all. For where, indeed, shall I be when I shall be no
more? Can it be death? No, I will not die." He sprang up and
would have lit the candle, fumbled about with tremulous
hands, upset the candle and candlestick on to the floor, and
again fell back on his pillow. "Why bother? It is all one," he
said to himself, gazing into the darkness with open eyes.
"Death? Yes, death, and they know nothing about it, and don't
want to know, and have no pity. They are playing." (He heard
far away, beyond the door, the sound of voices and music.) "It
is all one to them, and yet they must die too. The fools! 'Twill
be a little sooner for me and a little later for them, that's all; it
will be all the same in the end. And they are happy. Brutes!"
He was suffocated with rage. And he was in torments and un-
endurably wretched. "Can it be that everyone is doomed to experience this dreadful anguish?" He got up.

"I ought not to go on like this, I ought to be calm and think
over everything from the beginning." And so he began to re-
flect. "Yes, the disease began like that I bumped my side, and it
remained much about the same as before both that day and
the day after. Then I had a dull sort of pain, and then it got a

little worse, then I had the doctor, and then came low spirits and anguish, and then the doctor again, and all the time I was drawing nearer and nearer to the abyss. My strength begins to fail. Nearer and nearer. And now I dwindle to nothing, and there is no light in my eyes. It is death, and here am I only thinking of my bowels! I am thinking how to set my bowels in order, and it is death that is knocking at my door. Can it really be death?"

And again terror seized him; he panted for breath, bent over and began to search for the candle, and knocked the little pedestal-table beside him with his elbow. It stood in his way and hurt him; he flew into a passion with it, pressed upon it still harder in his anger, and overturned the pedestaltable. And in despair, and gasping for breath, he rolled back upon his back awaiting death immediately.

The guests were departing at that very time. Praskov'ya Thedorovna was showing them out. She heard the fall and went in.

"What's the matter?"

"Nothing. I have let something fall unexpectedly."

She went out and brought a light. There he lay, breathing rapidly and heavily, like a man who had run a mile, looking at her with glazing eyes.

"What is the matter, Jean?"

"No—no—nothing. It drop—ped. —What can I say? She will not understand," he thought to himself.

And, indeed, she did not understand. She got up, lit his candle, and went out hastily. She had to take leave of a guest. When she came back he was lying on his back gazing at the ceiling.

"How are you? — worse, eh?"

"Yes."

She shook her head and sat down.

"I tell you what, Jean, hadn't we better send and see if Lesh-chetetsky is at home?"

That meant telling the famous doctor to call, and not sparing their money. He smiled bitterly and said no. After sitting a little longer she approached him and kissed him on the forehead.

At that moment he hated her with all the strength of his soul, and with difficulty refrained from repulsing her.

"Good-bye. God grant you may get a little sleep."

"Yes."

CHAPTER VI

Ivan Il'ich saw that he was dying, and despaired continually.

In the depth of his soul he knew that he was dying, but not only did he not become accustomed to it, but he simply could not understand it — could not understand it at all.

That syllogism which he had learnt in Kizeveter's logic: "Caius is a man, all men are mortal, therefore Caius is mortal," had seemed to him, all his life long, to apply only to Caius, and to have no reference to himself. Gaius was a man, man in general, and it was quite correct as applied to Caius; but he was not Caius, he was not man in general; he had always been quite, quite distinct from all other creatures. Yes, he was Jack with his own mamma and papa, and with Mita and Voloda and his playthings and his coachman and his nurse, and afterwards with his Kitty, and with all the joys, sorrows, and triumphs of childhood, boyhood, and youth. What had Caius to do with the smell of that striped leather ball that he, Jack, loved so much? Did Caius ever kiss the hand of a mother as he had done? Did Caius ever hear the crinkling of the folds of his mother's silk dress? Did Caius ever smuggle in tarts during a lesson in jurisprudence? Was Caius ever in love? Could Caius ever have presided in Court ?

And Caius was certainly mortal, and must die in the regular course of things; but as for me, Vanya, Ivan Il'ich, with all my feelings and sentiments — that's quite a different thing. It cannot possibly be that I must die, that would be too terrible.

Thus did he think within himself.

"If I had to die like Caius, then I should have known it, then an inner voice must needs have told me so; but there was nothing of the sort within me, and I and all my friends quite understood that we were quite different from Caius. And now look here! "he said to himself." It cannot be, it cannot be, and yet it is. What's the meaning of it? How shall I understand it?"

And he could not understand it, and tried to drive the thought away from him as a false, abnormal, morbid thought, and to substitute for it other normal, healthy thoughts. But this thought, and it was not a mere thought, but as if a reality, came to him again and remained constantly before him.

And he summoned one after the other to take the place of this thought other thoughts, hoping to find a support in them. He tried to return to his former habit of thought which had formerly obscured from him the thought of death; but, strange to say, all that had formerly obscured, concealed, annihilated the thought of death, was unable now to produce that effect. Of late Ivan Il'ich had spent a considerable time in these attempts to revive those "habits of thought which had obscured the thought of death. "At one time," he said, "I will get absorbed in my official business, I really live for that." And he had gone to Court driving away from him all doubts; he had entered into conversation with his colleagues, and would sit in his old way, distraught, skimming over the crowd with a dreamy look, and with both his hands, growing meagre now, resting on the arm of his oak chair, and, as usual, he would bend over to the colleague who was opening the case and whisper a few words to him, and then, suddenly looking up and sitting straight in his chair, would pronounce certain words and begin the business. But suddenly, in the midst of it all, the pain in the side, paying no heed to the development of the case, would begin its sucking action. Ivan Il'ich, becoming aware of it, would drive the thought of it away from him, but it went on with its business, and it came forward and stood right in front of him, and looked at him, and he was turned to stone, the fire of his eye was extinguished, and he began again to ask himself: I wonder whether it alone is right? And his colleagues and his subordinates noticed with astonishment and indignation how he, the brilliant, subtle judge, was getting confused and making blunders. Then he would grow alarmed and try and fix his attention, and try, somehow or other, to hold out till the end of the session, and would return home with the bitter consciousness that his business in Court could no longer hide from him what he wanted to be hidden, that his business in Court could not deliver him from it. And worse than all else was this: it drew him towards it, not in order that he might do something, but simply that he might look at it, straight into its eyes, look at it, and helplessly inert, be inexpressibly tormented.

And escaping from this condition of mind, Ivan Il'ich would seek relief by interposing other screens between him and it, and these other screens would present themselves and for a time seem to deliver him, but immediately they would not so much be destroyed as become transparent, as if it was shining through everything, and nothing whatever could guard against it.

Once during these latter days he went into the drawing-room arranged by him, that very drawing-room where he had had the fall, for the sake of which — oh, the bitterly ridiculous thought of it! — for the sake of arranging which he had sacrificed his life, for he knew that his malady began with the contusion he had received there; well, he entered the room and perceived that there was a dent in the japanned table, cut deep in by something or other. He sought for the cause of it, and found it in the bronze ornamentation of the album which had been bent back at the corner. He took the album, a dear one, which he himself had introduced there con amore, and was very angry at the carelessness of his daughter and her friends; this thing torn too, these visiting cards all scattered about. He very carefully put everything in order again, and bent back the ornamentation of the album into its proper place.

On another occasion the idea occurred to him to move all this arrangement with the albums over into another corner where the flowers were. He called the lackey; either his daughter or his wife came to his assistance. They did not agree with him, they contradicted him; he wrangled, got angry, but it all did him good, because he had forgotten all about it, it was not visible.

But then his wife said, just when he was moving the things about with his own hands: "Allow me, let the servants do it, you will only do yourself harm again," and immediately it flashed through the screen, he saw it. It flashed through, and yet he made believe that it was hidden, but involuntarily he became attentive to his side again—there sat all the same old thing with the same dull old pain, and he could forget no longer, and it was plainly looking at him from behind the flowers. What was the good of it all?

"Yes, no doubt of it, on this curtain, just as much as if I had been storming a breach, did I lose my life. Can it be possible? How horrible and how stupid! It cannot be! It cannot be, yet it is."

He went into his cabinet, lay down, and once more was alone with it. Eye to eye with it, and to come to terms with it—impossible. He could only look at it and grow cold.

CHAPTER VII

How it happened in the third month of the illness of Ivan Il'ich it is impossible to say, because it happened insensibly, step by step, but at any rate this thing did happen: his wife, his daughter, his son, his servants, his acquaintances, the doctor, and especially he himself, knew that the sole interest felt in him by others was as to how soon he would finally vacate his place, release the living from the impediment of his existence, and deliver himself from his sufferings.

He got less and less sleep; they gave him opium and began to inject morphia. But this did not relieve him. The dull anguish which he experienced in his semi-conscious condition at first was a simple relief from its very novelty, but subsequently it became just as tormenting, and even more tormenting than open pain.

They prepared for him special dishes by the doctor's directions, but all these dishes struck him as being more and more tasteless, more and more nauseating.

In order to assist his evacuations, special apparatuses were arranged, and every time they were applied it was a torture to him. And this torture was increased by the consciousness that another man had to take part in it.

Yet this very unpleasant business itself brought some relief to Ivan Il'ich. The person who always had to do these things for him was the man-servant, Gerasim.

Gerasim was a clean, fresh young muzhik, always bright and merry. At first the sight of this ever cleanly young fellow, dressed in the Russian fashion, performing this disgusting office, deeply distressed Ivan Il'ich.

Once when he had risen from the night-stool without strength enough to draw up his pantaloons, he had sunk into a soft chair, and gazed with horror upon his exposed impotent calves, with their sharply defined muscles.

At that moment Gerasim entered in thick boots, distributing around him a pleasant smell of tar from his boots and of fresh winter air, walking with a light, strong step in a clean linen blouse and a clean cotton shirt, with his sleeves turned up over his naked, strong young arms, and not looking at Ivan Il'ich, and visibly restraining, so as not to offend the invalid, his sensation of the joy of life which was beaming in his face, went towards the close-stool.

"Gerasim!" said Ivan Il'ich feebly.

Gerasim trembled, evidently fearing lest he might have committed some blunder or other, and with a quick movement turned towards the invalid his fresh, good, simple young face, on which a beard was just beginning to sprout

"What do you want, sir?"

"I am afraid this is an unpleasant job for you. Forgive me, I cannot help it."

"Lord, help us!" cried Gerasim with sparkling eyes, and showing his young, white teeth as he smiled; "why shouldn't I do this little job? You are so bad, sir."

And with his strong, skilful arms he performed his usual office, and went out with a light step. And in five minutes he came back again, stepping just as lightly as before.

Ivan Il'ich was still sitting in the chair.

"Gerasim," said he, when the latter had replaced the clean, well-washed close-stool, "come hither, if you please, and help me."

Gerasim came.

"Lift me up. It is hard for me alone, and I have sent Dmitry away."

Gerasim came. With his strong arms, just as lightly as he had walked, he embraced Ivan Il'ich skilfully, lifted him up softly, and, holding him up, with the other hand he readjusted his pantaloons, and would have set him down again. But Ivan Il'ich begged him to carry him to the divan. Gerasim without an effort, and as if he scarce held him, led him, almost carrying him to the divan, and sat him down upon it.

"Thanks, how well and cleverly you do everything."

Gerasim smiled again and would have gone away, but Ivan Il'ich liked to be with him so much that he did not want to dismiss him.

"Push that chair yonder close up to me, if you please. No, that one there — under my legs. I feel easier when my legs are raised."

Gerasim brought the chair, placed it in position without knocking it against anything, and placed Ivan Il'ich's feet upon it. It seemed to Ivan Il'ich that he felt much easier ever since Gerasim had raised his feet higher.

"I feel easier when my feet are higher," said Ivan Il'ich. " Place that cushion there under me."

Gerasim did so. Again he raised Ivan Il'ich's feet and placed the cushion. Again Ivan Il'ich felt better so long as Gerasim held up his feet.

As soon as he let them go he felt worse.

"Gerasim," he said to him, " have you got employment now?"

"No, none at all," said Gerasim, who had been learning from the townspeople how to speak with gentlemen.

"What else have you got to do besides this?"

"What have I got to do? I have done everything now, I have only got to chop wood for to-morrow."

"Then go on holding my feet up a little higher — can you?"

"Why of course." Gerasim raised the feet higher. And it seemed to Ivan Il'ich as if in this position he didn't feel the pain at all.

"And how about that wood, eh?"

"Pray do not be uneasy about it, we'll manage."

Ivan Il'ich ordered Gerasim to sit down and hold his feet, and he talked to him. And it was a strange thing, but it seemed to him that he was better so long as Gerasim held his feet

From henceforth Ivan Il'ich used sometimes to call Gerasim, and get him to hold his feet on his shoulders, and loved to talk with him. Gerasim did this easily, willingly, simply, and so good-naturedly that Ivan Il'ich was touched by it. Health, strength, fulness of life in all other people offended Ivan Il'ich, but strength and fulness of life in Gerasim did not fret but soothed Ivan Il'ich.

The chief torment of Ivan Il'ich was falsehood, the falsehood adopted in some way or other by them all, that he was only ill and not dying, and that all he had to do was to keep quiet and get well, and then it would be all right. He knew very well that whatever they might do, nothing would come of it but still greater torments and death. And this lie tormented him; it tormented him that they would not recognise what they knew and what he knew to be a fact, but would lie to him about his terrible position, and wanted him to, and made him, participate in this lie.

Lies, lies, all these lies lied about him up to the very eve of his death; lies which were bound to degrade this terrible, solemn act of his death down to the level of all their visits, curtains, caviare for dinner—this was a terrible torment for Ivan Il'ich. And it was a strange thing that many a time, when they were fooling him like this, he was within a hair's-breadth of shrieking at them: "Enough of this falsehood. You know, and I know, that I am dying, so at any rate cease to lie about it." But he never had the heart to do this. The frightful, terrible act of his dying—he could see it plainly—was degraded by all who surrounded him to the level of a temporary unpleasantness, an indecency (of the same sort as how to avoid a man who on entering a drawing-room disseminates a bad odour), being so degraded by that same sense of "decency" to which he himself had been a slave all his life, he perceived that none pitied him because none even wanted to understand his condition. Only Gerasim understood that condition, and was sorry for him. And therefore it was only well with Ivan Il'ich when he was with Gerasim.

It was well with him when Gerasim, sometimes whole nights at a stretch, held up his feet, and would not go to sleep, saying: "Pray do not put yourself about, Ivan Il'ich, sleep a little more;" or, when suddenly addressing him with the familiar thou, added: "As if thou wert not ill, and why should not I render thee this little service?"

Gerasim alone told no lies, everything showed that he alone knew how the matter stood, and did not consider it necessary to conceal it, and was simply sorry for his weak, expiring master. On one occasion, when Ivan Il'ich was for sending him away, he spoke right out: "We must all die, why shouldn't I take a little trouble? " said he, thereby expressing that he made light of his labour, principally because he was doing it for the sake of a dying man, and hoped that for him also someone would do the same sort of work when his time came.

Besides this sort of lying, or in consequence of it, the most tormenting thing of all for Ivan Il'ich was the fact that nobody pitied him as he wanted to be pitied; at certain times, after long suffering, the wish would come to Ivan Il'ich, though he would not willingly have admitted it, that someone might pity him just as if he were a sick child, and it was the thing he wished for most of all. He wished that they would caress him and kiss him and weep over him a little, just as people caress and soothe children. He knew that he was an important functionary, that he had a grizzling beard, and therefore that it was impossible, and yet he wished it all the same. In his relations with Gerasim there was something akin to this. And therefore his relations with Gerasim soothed him. Ivan Il'ich wanted to weep, and he wanted others to caress him and weep over him;

and then his colleague, the functionary Shebek, comes to see him, and instead of weeping and allowing himself to be caressed, Ivan Il'ich puts on a serious, severe, profound expression of face, and, as far as his inertia will allow him, delivers his opinion on the significance of the judgments of the Court of Appeal, and obstinately clings to the subject. This lie, all around him, and within himself, envenomed more than anything else the last days of the life of Ivan Il'ich.

CHAPTER VIII

It was morning. It was only morning because Gerasim went away, and Peter the lackey appeared, extinguished the candles, opened one of the curtains, and began very quietly to tidy up the room. Whether it was morning or evening, or Friday or Sunday — it didn't matter which — it was all one and the same thing: the dull, dragging, torturing pain, never for an instant still, the hopeless consciousness of a life that was constantly ebbing, but had not yet quite ebbed away; the consciousness of death, the hateful and terrible, ever-advancing death, the one reality, and yet all this lying going on at the same time. How could there be any talk here of days or weeks, or the days of the week?

"Did you order tea, sir?"

It is a necessary rule that the gentry should drink tea in the morning, he thought to himself, but he only said no.

"Would you like to be moved on to the divan, sir?"

He has to put the bedroom in order, and I am in the way, and I am dirt and disorder, he thought to himself, but all he said was: "No, leave me."

The lackey still kept bustling about. Ivan Il'ich stretched out his hand. Peter approached obsequiously. "Do you want anything, sir?" "My watch."

Peter got the watch, lying under his very arm, and gave it to him. "Half-past nine. Are they up?" "No, sir. Vladimir Ivanovich (that was his son) has gone to the gymnasium, but Praskov'ya Thedorovna commanded that they should be awakened if you asked for anything. Did you want them, sir?"

"No, it is not necessary." Shall I try a little tea? he thought "Yes, bring me some tea."

Peter went towards the door. It was a terrible thing to Ivan Il'ich to be left alone. How should he keep the servant a little longer? Yes, there was his medicine.

"Peter, give me my medicine." The medicine might do him good after all, there was no knowing. He took the spoon and drank it. No, it was no good. It's all nonsense, deception, he decided, as soon as ever he had tasted the familiar, nasty, and hopeless stuff. No, I can believe in it no longer. But this pain, this pain, why should I have it? If only it would stop for an instant. And he groaned. Peter turned round. "No, go, bring the tea."

Peter departed. Ivan Il'ich, left alone, groaned, not so much from pain, horrible as it was, as from weariness. It was always the same thing over again, all these endless days and nights. If only it would be quicker. Quicker? What did he mean? Death, darkness. No, no. Anything was better than death.

When Peter came in with the tea on a tray, Ivan Il'ich looked at him absently for a long time, not comprehending who he was or what he was. Peter grew confused at this steadfast gaze, and when Peter was confused Ivan Il'ich came to himself again.

"Ah!" said he, "the tea. Very well, put it down, only help me to wash and put on a clean shirt."

And Ivan Il'ich began to wash. Breathing heavily, he washed his hands, his face, cleaned his teeth, began to comb his hair and to look at himself in the mirror. It was a terrible thing to him, a peculiarly terrible thing, to note how closely his hair clung to his pale forehead.

When he came to change his shirt, he knew that it would be still more dreadful for him if he looked at his body, so he did not look at it. But it was finished at last. He put on a dressing-gown, wrapped a plaid round him, and sat down in his chair to tea. For a moment he felt himself refreshed, but no sooner had he begun to drink the tea than that taste, that pain, came back again. With an effort he finished the tea and lay down, stretching out his legs. He lay down and dismissed Peter.

It was the same thing over again. At one moment a gleam of hope, the next moment a raging sea of despair, and all was pain, pain, misery, misery, and the same thing over and over again. All this lonely misery was terrible; he would have liked to send for someone or other, but he knew beforehand that it was still worse when other people were with him. "If only I might have some more morphine, I might forget about it I shall tell the doctor that he must invent something else. To go on like this is impossible, quite impossible."

An hour or two passed in this way. But now there came a ring at the vestibule. The doctor perhaps? Yes, it was the doctor — fresh, brisk, plump, merry, with that sort of expression which says: Ah! ha! we are a little bit nervous, eh? but we'll very soon put all that to rights. The doctor knows that this expression is quite out of place here, but he has put it on once for all and cannot lay it aside again, like a man who has put on a frock-coat in the morning to go visiting.

The doctor came in rubbing his hands in a brisk, encouraging fashion.

"I'm cold, there's a healthy frost to-day; let me warm myself a bit," he exclaimed, as much as to say you must wait a little bit till I have warmed myself, and when once I have warmed myself I'll very soon put things to rights.

"Well now, how are we ?"

Ivan Il'ich felt that what the doctor really wanted to say was: How is our little affair going on? but that feeling it was impossible to say this he said instead: How are we getting on? by which he meant to say: What sort of a night have you had?

Ivan Il'ich looked at the doctor with an expression of face which really asked him: "Will you never be ashamed of telling lies, I wonder?" but the doctor would not notice the inquiry.

Then Ivan Il'ich said: "Just as badly as ever; the pain won't go away, and never ceases. If only you could give me something."

"That's always the way with you invalids. I'm now pretty well warmed, I think. Even Praskov'ya Thedorovna, who is always so careful, could make no objection to my temperature now. Well now, let's see, how are you?" And the doctor pressed his hand.

And now, forsaking his former sprightliness, the doctor, with a serious face, began to examine the patient, feel his pulse, take his temperature, tap him, and put his ear to him.

Ivan Il'ich was firmly and indubitably persuaded that all this was nonsense and pure deceit, but when the doctor, going down on his knees, bent over him and glued his ear to him, now higher up and now lower down, and, with a most important countenance, made various gymnastic evolutions over him, Ivan Il'ich submitted to it as he had submitted to the speeches of advocates in court, knowing very well all the time that they were lying all the time, and why they were lying.

The doctor was still on his knees at the divan, and still poking away at Ivan Il'ich when the silk dress of Praskov'ya Thedorovna rustled in the doorway, and they could hear her reproaching Peter for not telling her that the doctor had arrived.

She came in, kissed her husband, and immediately began to prove that she had been up long ago, and that it was only owing to a misunderstanding that she had not been there when the doctor arrived

Ivan Il'ich looked at her, and took her all in, and her whiteness and her puffiness, and the cleanness of her hands and neck, and the glitter of her hair, and the brightness of her eyes full of life, were all so many causes of reproach against her. He hated her with all the force of his soul, and her mere contact made him suffer from an access of hatred against her.

Her attitude towards him and his illness was precisely the same. Just as the doctor had taken up an attitude towards the sick man which he could not now drop, so, too, she had taken up an attitude towards him, founded on the assumption that he would not do anything he ought to do, and it was all his own fault, and she loved to blame him for it, and this attitude once taken up she could not drop it.

"He wouldn't listen, you know; he wouldn't take things in time, and, above all, he lies in a position which is very bad for him, with his legs up."

And she told the doctor how he had made Gerasim hold his feet up.

The doctor smiled with bland contemptuousness.

"What are we to do?" said he; "these invalids, you know, sometimes do have such odd ideas, but we may forgive him, I suppose."

When the examination was completed, the doctor looked at his watch, and then Praskov'ya Thedorovna told Ivan Il'ich that she had done what he wanted, and invited the famous doctor to come and see him, and they, together with Mikhail Danilovich (that was the name of the general practitioner), were to examine him and form an opinion.

"You surely will not object, I am doing this on my own account," she said ironically, giving him to understand that hitherto she had done everything as he wanted it, and that only in this instance she would not allow him to refuse her. He was silent and frowned. He felt that this lie enveloping him was so complicated that it would be very, difficult to put anything right.

And, indeed, at half-past twelve the famous doctor arrived. Again there were auscultations and grave consultations in his apartment and in another apartment, and a lot of talk about the kidneys and the intestines, and questions and answers with such important looks that, once more, instead of the real question of life and death, which was now alone impending over him, a new question emerged about the kidneys and the intestines, which, somehow or other, were not acting as they ought to do, and upon which organs, in consequence, Mikhail Danilovich and the medical celebrity fell at once, and made up their minds to put them to rights.

The celebrated doctor took his leave with a serious but not a hopeless expression of countenance, and, in reply to the audacious question which Ivan Il'ich put to him, at the same time fixing him with eyes sparkling with terror and hope, namely, whether there was any possibility of a cure, the celebrated doctor replied that he couldn't guarantee it, but that it was possible. The look of hope with which Ivan Il'ich followed the doctor out was so piteous that, on perceiving it, Praskov'ya Thedorovna burst into tears as she passed through the door of the cabinet to give the celebrated doctor his honorarium.

The good spirits, caused by the encouragement of the doctor, did not last long. There was the same room, there were the same pictures, the same curtains, furniture, vases, and that self-same sick and suffering body of his. And Ivan Il'ich began to groan; they gave him an injection and he forgot everything. When he came to himself again it was beginning to be dusk, and they brought him his dinner. With an effort he ate a little of the soup; it was all the same over again, and then came nightfall as usual.

After dinner at seven o'clock, Praskov'ya Thedorovna came into his room, in evening dress, with her stout, protuberant bosom, and traces of powder on her face. That very morning she had reminded him that they were going to the theatre. It was Sarah Bernhardt's benefit, and they had a box which he had insisted upon their taking. Now he had forgotten all about this, and her get-up offended him. But he concealed his vexation when he remembered that he himself had insisted that they should hire the box and go, because it would be an intellectual, aesthetic treat for the children.

Praskov'ya Thedorovna came in well satisfied with herself, and yet with a guilty air. She sat down beside him and asked him how he was, simply for the sake of asking, as he could see, and not for the sake of finding out, knowing very well that there was nothing to find out. Then she began to say that she was bound to go, though she would give anything not to go; but the box was taken and Elen was going and his daughter, and Petrishchev (the judicial assessor, his daughter's fiancé) and that it was impossible to let them go alone, but that it would have been much more agreeable to her to sit at home with him, only he was to promise to obey the doctor's directions during her absence.

"Yes, and Thedor Dmitrievich (the fiancè) would like to come in and see him. Might he come? And Liza?"

"Let them come in if they like."

His daughter came in dressed up, with her bare young body, the same sort of body which was causing him all his suffering, and she showed him her dress. A strong, healthy young girl, visibly in love with herself, and disgusted with disease, suffering, and death, as interfering with her happiness.

Thedor Dmitrievich also came in in a dress coat, with his hair curled à la capoul, with a long, sinewy neck encircled by a white linen collar, with an enormous white shirt front and narrow black trousers, with a tight-fitting white glove on one hand, and an opera hat

After him crept in, unobserved, the gymnasiast, also, in his new little uniform, poor little wretch, in gloves, and with frightful blue lines under his eyes, the significance of which Ivan Il'ich knew very well.

He had always felt sorry for his son, and it was terrible to behold his frightened and compassionate look. Except Gerasim, it seemed to Ivan Il'ich as if Voloda alone understood and pitied him.

They all sat down, again they asked him about his health. Silence ensued. Liza asked her mother about the opera glass. There was a slight dispute between mother and daughter as to what had become of it. The dispute ended unpleasantly.

Theodor Dmitrievich asked Ivan Il'ich whether he had seen Sarah Bernhardt Ivan Il'ich did not at first understand the question, and presently answered no.

"You have seen her already, I suppose?"

"Yes, in 'Adrienne Lecouvreur.' "

Praskov'ya Thedorovna said that she was particularly good in that part. The daughter contradicted. An argument began about the elegance and realism of her acting, that sort of conversation which is always one and the same thing.

In the middle of the conversation Theodor Dmitrievich looked at Ivan Il'ich and was silent. The others looked at him and were silent Ivan Il'ich was gazing in front of him with sparkling eyes, evidently he was angry with them. Evidently this ought to be put right, but there was no means whatever of putting it right. This silence ought to be broken somehow. But nobody could make up his mind to do so, and it was frightfully awkward to all of them that no convenient lie was ready to hand, and it was plain to all of them what was wanted. Liza was the first to make up her mind. She broke the silence. She wanted to conceal what all of them were experiencing, but she spoke out.

"Well, if we must go, it's high time," she said, looking at her watch, a gift from her father, and smiling at her young man with a scarcely noticeable significant look, which he alone understood, and she stood up rustling her dress.

Then they all stood up, said good-bye, and went away.

When they had gone out, Ivan Il'ich felt a little easier; the lie was no longer there, it had gone out with them, but the pain remained. The same continual pain, the same continual terror had this effect, that nothing was heavier, nothing was lighter, everything was for the worst.

Again, minute after minute, hour after hour, passed by; it was the same thing over and over again, and there was no end to it, and more terrible than all was the inevitable end.

"Yes, send Gerasim here," he replied to a question from Peter.

CHAPTER IX

Late at night his wife returned ; she came in on tip- toe, but he heard her, opened his eyes, and quickly closed them again. She wanted to send away Gerasim and sit with him herself. He opened his eyes and said : " No, go away."

" You are suffering very much, eh ? "

" Much the same as usual."

" Take some opium."

He consented, and drank it. She went out.

For about three hours he was in a tormenting slumber. It seemed to him as if he and the pain were shut up together somehow in a narrow and deep black sack, and were getting deeper and deeper into it and couldn't get out And this hor-

rible state of affairs was accompanied with great personal suf-
fer- ing. And he was afraid, and wanted to break out somewhere and struggled, and wanted help. And quite suddenly
he burst out of the sack and fell somewhere, and awoke. Gerasim was still sitting at his feet on the bed, brooding quietly
and patiently. There he was lying with the thin, stockinged
feet of his master raised upon his shoulders ; the light was still
there with the shade upon it, and there, too, was the same un-
ceasing pain.

" Go away, Gerasim," he whispered.

" It doesn't matter, I'll sit a bit longer."

" No, go away."

He removed his feet, lay with his hand on his side, and felt
very sorry for himself. He continued to lie like this until Gerasim had gone into the other room, and then he was unable to
contain himself, and wept like a child. He wept because of his
helplessness, because of his frightful loneliness, because of the
cruelty of people, because of the cruelty of God, because of the
absence of God.

"Why hast Thou done all this? Why hast Thou brought me
hither ? Why, oh why, dost Thou torture me so terribly ? "

He did not expect an answer, and he wept because there
was no answer, and couldn't be an answer. The pain rose up
again, but he did not move, he did not call. He said to himself:
"Very well, then, smite me ! But what for ? What have I done
to Thee ? Why dost Thou smite me ? "

After that he was silent, he ceased not only to weep, but
even to breathe, and became all attention, as if he were listening not to the voice which speaks through the lips, but to the
voice of the soul, to the current of thought arising up within
him.

"What dost thou require?" was the first clear notion express-
ible by words which he heard.

"What dost thou require?" he kept repeating to himself. " What ? Not to suffer. To live," he answered.

And again he gave himself up entirely to an attentive expectation, so intense that even his pain did not distract him.

" To live ? How do you mean to live ? " asked the voice of the soul.

" To live as I lived before, well and pleasantly."

" As you lived before, well and pleasantly ? " asked the voice.

And he began to go over in his imagination the best moments of his pleasant life. But, oddly enough, all these best moments of his pleasant life seemed to him to be quite different now to what they had seemed then. It was so with all of them except the recollections of his childhood. There in his childhood there was something really pleasant, with which it was possible to live if only he could go back to it. But there was now no trace of the man who had experienced this pleasantness, it was like a reminiscence of someone else.

No sooner did he begin to consider what was the result of his life, namely, that actually present he, Ivan Il'ich, than everything that had seemed so pleasant thawed away before his very eyes and turned into nothingness, a nothingness that was sometimes odious.

And the further away he got from his childhood, and the nearer he drew to the present time, the more insignificant and doubtful this pleasantness became. This began from the time that he was a law student. Then, indeed, there was still something that was really good; then there was gaiety, then there was friendship, then there were hopes. But in the higher classes these good moments became rarer and rarer. Afterwards, in the time of his first service at the Governor's, there were again some good moments ; these were the recollections of his love for his wife. Afterwards all this was mixed up, and there was still less of good in it Still further on there was still less of good, and the further he went on the less of good he found.

Then came his marriage — and disillusionment so unexpectedly . . . and the sensuality of it and the hypocrisy ! And this dead officialism, and this care about money, and then a year of it, and two years of it, and ten, and twenty — and always the same old thing over again! And the further it went on the more it savoured of death. "And I going down- hill so nonchalantly, imagining all the time that I was going uphilL And so it was. According to the general opinion I was going uphill, and all the time life was just as much vanishing from beneath me. And now I am ready. Let me die !

"Why is it all so? Why, indeed? It cannot be! It cannot be that life is so senseless, so hideous? And if it really was so odious and senseless, why die, and die suffering? There is something not right."

Possibly I have not lived as I ought to have lived? flashed through his head. But how can that be when I have always done my duty? And immediately he drove away from him this unique solution of all the riddles of life and death, as if it were something absolutely impossible.

And what do you want now? To live? How? To live as you lived in the Courts when the court-usher announced: "Judgment is going to be de-livered!"

"Judgment is coming, judgment is coming," he kept repeating to himself. "Is this the judgment? And I am surely not guilty ! " he cried aloud with rage. "What for?" And he ceased to weep, and turning his face to the wall kept thinking continually of one and the same thing : " Wherefore all this horror ? "

But think of it as he might, he could find no answer. And when, as it frequently did come, the thought came to him that all this arose from the circumstance that he had not lived as he ought to have lived, he immediately called to mind the regular life he had always led, and drove away that frightful thought.

CHAPTER X

Another fortnight had passed. Ivan Il'ich was now confined to the divan. He would not lie in bed, but he lay on the divan. And lying almost the whole time with his face to the wall, he suffered continually in his solitude the same inexplicable sufferings, and kept on thinking the same inexplicable thought : " What is this ? Can it be true that this is death?" And the inner voice answered: "Yes, it is true." — " Wherefore these torments?" — It is because, not wherefore. Besides and beyond this there was nothing at all.

From the very beginning of his illness, from the time that Ivan Il'ich first went to the doctor, his life had been divided between two opposite inter- changing tendencies — on the one hand despair and the expectation of an unintelligible and terrible death ; on the other hand hope and the absorbingly interesting observation of the natural processes of his body; on the one hand was an unintelligible, terrible death, from which there was absolutely no escape ; and, on the other hand, there was constantly before his eyes his bowels or his kidneys, which temporarily refused to perform their proper functions.

From the very beginning of his illness these two tendencies were continually superseding each other ; but the further the disease advanced the more dubious and fantastic became the physiological ideas, and the more real the consciousness of approaching death.

He had only to remember what he had been three months before and what he was now — he had only to remember how steadily he had been going down- hill, in order to destroy every possibility of hope.

During the latter period of the loneliness in which he was, lying with his face turned to the back of the divan, that loneliness in the midst of the populous city, and his numerous acquaintances and their families, a loneliness more complete than any loneliness to be found elsewhere, whether it were to be sought in the bottom of the sea or in the earth — in the latter period of this frightful loneliness Ivan Il'ich lived in imagination entirely in the past One after another the pictures of his past life presented themselves before him. It always began with what was nearest in time and went on to what was most distant — to his childhood, and there stopped. When Ivan Il'ich thought of the preserved plums which they were giving him to eat now, he called to mind a moist, wrinkled plum in his childhood, of its peculiar taste, and of how his mouth watered when he got down to the kernel, and along with this recollection of the taste of the plum there arose a whole series of other recollections of the same period — his nurse, his brother, his playthings. "But I mustn't think of that, it is too painful," said Ivan Il'ich to himself, and again he transferred his thoughts to the present time. The buttons on the back of the divan, and the wrinkles of the morocco reminded him of something else. " Morocco is dear, it wont last," his wife had said, " and there had been a quarrel about that. But the morocco was another morocco, and there was another quarrel " when we tore papa's portfolio, and they punished us, and mamma brought us cakes." And again he lingered over his child- hood, and again it was painful to Ivan Il'ich, and he tried to drive it away and to think of something else*

And now again, together with this series of recollections, another series of recollections began to pass through his mind as to how his disease had grown and increased. It was the same thing; the further back he went the more of life there was.

There was also more of good in life, and life itself was fuller. And both these recollections blended together. As the torments kept on growing worse and worse, so also all life grew worse and worse, he thought to himself. There was a bright point far back in the beginning of life, and after that everything was blacker and blacker and quicker and quicker. "The pace is in inverse proportion to the distance from death," thought Ivan Il'ich to himself. And this image of a stone flying downwards with ever- increasing velocity fastened upon his mind. Life, a series of ever-increasing sufferings, was always flying more and more rapidly towards its end, and that end most frightful suffering. " I am flying. . . ." He trembled, writhed, would have resisted, but he knew already that it was no use resisting; and again, wearied of looking, yet unable not to look at what was before him, he gazed at the back of the divan, and waited and waited for that frightful fall, jolt, and destruction. " It's no good resisting," he said to himself, "yet if only I knew why this is, and that is impossible. It might be explained if I were to say that I have not lived as I ought to have lived, but this I cannot possibly acknowledge," said he to himself as he recollected all the correctness, regularity, and respectability of his life. "It is impossible to allow that," said he to himself, smiling with his lips as if someone could see this smile of his and be deceived by it "There is no explanation ! Torment, death. . . . Wherefore ? "y it.

"There is no explanation! Agony, death. . . . What for?"

CHAPTER XI

Thus a fortnight passed away. During this fortnight happened an event which Ivan Il'ich and his wife had long wished for. Petrishchev made a formal proposal for the hand of his daughter. This happened in the evening. Next day Praskov'ya Thedorovna went to her husband, meaning to tell him about the offer of Theodor Petrishchev, but that same night a change for the worse had taken place in the condition of Ivan Il'ich. Praskov'ya Thedorovna found him on the same sofa, but in a new position. He was lying on his back groaning, and gazing in front of him with a fixed, vacant look.

She began to speak about his medicine. He turned his look upon hen She did not finish what she had begun to say, such anger, especially against herself, was expressed in that look.

"For Christ's sake let me die in peace," he said.

She would have gone away, but at that moment her daughter also came in and asked him how he was. He looked at his daughter as he had looked at his wife, and in answer to her question about his health drily said to her that he would very soon relieve them all of his existence. They were both silent, sat down for a little, and then went away.

"How are we to blame ? " said Liza to her mother.

"We haven't done anything. I am sorry for papa, but why should he torment us? "

The doctor came at the usual time. Ivan Il'ich answered him u Yes " and " No," never once ceasing to regard him angrily, and at the end of the interview he said :

"You know very well that nothing can help, so leave it"

"We can relieve the suffering," said the doctor.

"Even that you can't do; leave it"

The doctor went into the drawing-room and told Praskov'ya Thedorovna that things were going very badly, and that there was only one thing — opium — which could relieve his sufferings, which must be terrible.

The doctor said that his physical sufferings were terrible, and that was true ; but still more terrible than his physical suf-

ferings were his moral sufferings, and in this was his chief torment

His moral sufferings were due to this circumstance: that
night, looking at the sleepy, good- natured face of Gerasim,
with its high cheek-bones, it suddenly came into his head:
"What if, in very deed, the whole of my life, my conscious life,
was not what it ought to be?"

It came into his head that what had seemed to him before an
utter impossibility, namely, that he had lived his life not as he
ought to have lived it, that this might really be true. It came
into his head that those scarcely noticed inclinations of his to
fight against that which the most highly placed people regarded as a sovereign good, that those scarcely noticed inclinations, which he had instantly driven away from him, might
after all have been the real things he should have lived for,
and that everything else might not have been so. And his official duties, and his theory of life, and his family, and his social
and official interests — all this might not have been the real
thing ; he tried to defend it all to himself. And suddenly he felt
all the weakness of what he was defending. And there was no
use defending it.

"And if it is so," he said to himself, " and I am departing
from life with the consciousness that I have ruined everything
that was given to me, and it is impossible to put it right again,
what then ? "

He lay on his back, and began to go over his whole life
anew.

When, in the morning, he saw the lackey and then his wife,
and then his daughter, and then the doctor, all their move-
ments, all their words, confirmed to him the terrible truth
which had been revealed to him in the night. He saw in them
himself and all that for which he had lived, and he saw plainly
that it was all not the real thing — it was all a frightful, im-
mense deception, obscuring both life and death. The con-

sciousness of this increased his physical sufferings tenfold. He groaned and flung himself about, and tore off his clothes ; they seemed to stifle and oppress him, and therefore he hated them.

They gave him a large dose of opium, he lost consciousness, but at dinner-time the whole thing began over again. He drove them all away from him, and tossed from side to side.

His wife came to him and said : " Jean, my darling, do this for me, for me. It can do no harm, and is often of use. Come, it is really nothing. People in health often do it"

He opened his eyes widely.

"What, to communicate, eh? Why? It is not . necessary. And besides "

She burst out weeping.

"Yes, my friend, I will call our priest, he is so kind."

"Excellent, very well," said he.

When the priest came and confessed him he was touched, felt a sort of relief from his doubts, and consequently from his sufferings, and for a moment hope came back to him. Again he began to think about his lower intestine and the possibility of curing it He communicated with tears in his eyes.

When they laid him down after communion he felt easier for a moment, and again a hope of life appeared. He began to think of the operation which lay before him. " I want to live, to live," he said to himself.

His wife came to ask him how he was. She said the usual words, and added :

"Now, don't you feel better?"

Without looking at her he answered : " Yes."

Her dress, her attitude, the expression of her face, the sound of her voice — it all said to him this one thing: "All that which you have lived for, and would live for, is a lie and a deception, hiding from you life and death." And no sooner had he thought this than a hatred of it all rose up within him, and together with the hatred, physical torment, and with the torment the consciousness of inevitable, imminent ruin.

The expression of his face when he had said "Yes" was terrible. On pronouncing this yes he looked her straight in the face, and with extraordinary quickness, considering his weakness, he turned over on one side and cried : " Go away, go away, leave me."

CHAPTER XII

From that moment commenced the shrieking fit which lasted for three days, and was so terrible that it was impossible to hear it without horror even through two doors. When he had answered his wife he understood that he was lost, that there could be no return to health, that the end had come, quite the end, and although his doubt was now settled, yet doubt it remained.

" Wo ! Wo ! Wo ! " he cried in various intonations. He had begun with crying : " I won't, I won't," and then continued to cry the syllable " Wo " only.

These three days, during which time did not exist for him, he was struggling in that black sack into which an invisible, irresistible power had dragged him. He fought as a condemned criminal in the hands of the executioner fights, knowing that he cannot save himself, and every moment he felt that, notwithstanding all his struggles and exertion, he was drawing nearer and nearer to that which terrified him so. He felt that his torment consisted in his being dragged into this black hole, and still more in his being unable to creep through it. He was prevented from creeping through it by the consciousness that his life was good. This justification of his life held him as if with hooks, and would not let him get forward, and tormented him more than anything else.

Suddenly some sort of force smote him on the breast and in the side, his breathing became still more laboured, he struggled forward in the hole, and there at the end of the hole something or other was shining. He felt now as one feels in a railway carriage when one thinks that one is going forward when one is going backward, and one suddenly recognises the real direction.

"Yes, it was all what it should not have been," he said to himself, "but it doesn't matter. It is possible, quite possible, to do the right thing. But what is the right thing ? " he asked himself, and was again silent

This was at the end of the third day, two hours before his death. At this very time the gymnasiast had quietly crept into his father's room, and approached his bed. The dying man was still shrieking desperately and throwing his hands about. One of his hands fell on the head of the gymnasiast The little gymnasiast seized it, pressed it to his lips, and burst into tears.

At that same moment Ivan Il'ich came to himself, saw the light, and it was revealed to him that his life had not been what it ought to have been, but that it was still possible to set it right He asked himself: "What then is the right thing?" and was silent, listening intently. Then he felt that someone was kissing his hand. He opened his eyes and beheld his son. He was sorry for him. His wife approached him. There she was with open mouth, and with undried tears on her nose and cheek, regarding him with an expression of despair. He was sorry for her.

" Yes, I am tormenting them," he thought ; " it is wretched for them, but it will be better for them when I die." He wanted to say this, but he had not the strength to pronounce it "But why speak at all ? One must act," he thought to himself. With a look he indicated his son to his wife and said :

"Take away ... a pity . . . and thou also." He wanted to say besides : " Forgive," but he said : " Never mind," and not being strong enough to rectify the error he waved his hand, knowing that HE understood whom it alone concerned.

And suddenly it became clear to him that that which was tormenting him and would not go away was suddenly going away all at once and altogether. He was sorry for them, and he must cease from paining them. He must deliver them and deliver himself at the same time from these sufferings. " What a good and simple thing it is," he thought "And the pain," he asked himself, "whither has it gone? Come now, where art thou, oh pain?" He began to listen intently.

" Yes, there it is. Well, pain, thou mayest depart."

" And death, where is it ? "

He searched for his former habitual fear of death, and did not find it. " Where is it ? What is death ? " There was no terror because there was no death.

Instead of death there was light "Just look now ! " he suddenly cried aloud " What joy ! "

So far as he was concerned, all this had taken place in a single instant, and the insignificance of this instant remained unchanged So far as those present at his death-bed were concerned, his agony lasted another two hours. Something or other was heaving in his breast, his extenuated body was collapsing. Presently the heaving and gasping became less and less frequent

" It is all over," said somebody over him.

He heard these words and repeated them in his mind u Death is done with," he said to himself. M There is no more death."

He drew in his breath, uttered a half sigh, stretched himself and expired.

LEO TOLSTOY

All the light we
cannot see

CPSIA information can be obtained at www.ICGtesting.com
Printed in the USA
LVOW091954130612

286004LV00001B/49/P

9 781936 594665